November

Georges Simenon

November

Translated from the French by Jean Stewart

A Helen and Kurt Wolff Book

Harcourt Brace Jovanovich, Inc.

New York

First American edition

ISBN 0-15-167560-0
Library of Congress Catalog Card Number: 72-124826

Printed in the United States of America

November

1

I don't think I had ever seen anything like it before. It was the second Friday in November, November 9th to be exact. The four of us were sitting around the dinner table, as on any other evening. Manuela had just taken away the soup plates and brought in a *fines herbes* omelette, which my mother had gone into the kitchen to prepare.

Since morning, one of the fiercest storms of the whole year had been raging over France and the radio told of roofs being blown off, cars sent flying ten yards along the road, and ships lost in the Channel and in the Atlantic.

The wind was blowing in violent gusts that shook the house as though to uproot it, and the shutters, windows, and outer doors seemed about to give way at any moment.

The rain fell with relentless savagery, in heavy drifts, with a noise like waves breaking on a pebbled beach.

We none of us spoke. Our mealtimes are usually silent; only essential remarks are made.

"Would you mind passing me the dish, please?"

Each of us goes on eating, isolated from the others by an invisible wall, and that evening everyone was privately listening to the clamor of the storm.

Then suddenly, without warning, came silence; nature stood utterly still, and the emptiness was almost unbearable.

My father knit his bushy eyebrows. My brother stared at each of us in turn, with a look of surprise.

My mother imperceptibly tensed her long thin neck, as she glanced around mistrustfully. She is always suspicious of everything. She lives in a hostile universe, forever watchful, forever on the alert, with fixed gaze and straining neck like certain animals, certain birds of prey.

Nobody spoke. We all seemed to be holding our breath as though this sudden silence presaged some unknown disaster.

Only my father's expression, after that brief frown,

remained unchanged. His gray face seldom expresses more than a kind of solemn gravity.

Olivier glanced toward the door, which Manuela had just shut behind her, and I am convinced that he sent her a silent message. I am sure, too, that my mother intercepted that message without even turning her head. She sees and hears everything. She says nothing, but she takes mental note.

My brother soon recovered from the shock of the unexpected stillness of the world. He was sitting in his usual place opposite my father, and I was opposite my mother, who had those tell-tale red patches on her cheekbones.

It meant that she'd been drinking. She had started on her novena, as we call it, but she was not drunk, she's never really drunk.

"Are you feeling tired?"

Why did my father feel compelled to say that? She's no fool; she is far subtler than he is and she knows what words imply. This has been going on for so many years that there's no need for him to underline it.

"I've got my sick headache," she said curtly.

I don't know which of the two I pity more. It often seems as if my mother deliberately tries to be disagreeable, and even her silences have something aggressive about them. But could my father not be more easygoing, show a little understanding?

After all, he married her, and she cannot have been much better-looking then than she is now. I have seen photographs taken on their wedding day, in 1938. She has always been ill-favored; her nose is too long, with a sharp tip that seems to have been added as an afterthought, and her chin is too sharp too.

Was my father ever in love with her? Or was he merely proud, as a young lieutenant, to marry one of the daughters of his Colonel, who was shortly to become a General?

I know nothing about that. It's none of my business. It's not for me to judge them, although I can't help doing it. We live in a house where each of us watches the rest and leads a life apart. Only our Spanish maid Manuela, who has been with us two months, sings at her housework and behaves as if everything were quite normal around her.

Pears were served, and my father peeled his more carefully than the most accomplished *maître d'hôtel*. He does everything conscientiously, with a meticulousness that can be exasperating.

Does he feel obliged to restrain himself? Is there something artificial about his calm, dignified manner?

He rose from table first, as usual, just as he invariably sits down first and slowly unfolds his napkin. He has a sense of hierarchy, probably because he is an army man. That is also the reason, perhaps, why he attaches the same importance to small things as to great ones.

He muttered: "I'm going to do some work. . . ."

That's what he says almost every evening at the same time. He has turned one of the rooms, on the other side of the hall, into a study. In the middle there is an enormous nineteenth-century roll-top desk, and the glass-fronted bookcases are full of books and journals.

Does he really work there? He brings home a briefcase stuffed with papers from his office. We sometimes hear him tapping away unskillfully on his portable typewriter. More often, there's dead silence. We're supposed not to disturb him. Each of us is careful to knock if we happen to have something to say to him.

He has an old worn leather armchair in which I have often seen him sitting with his feet stretched out in front of the fireplace, where he has lighted a small wood fire. He lifts his head from his book and looks at you patiently, offering no encouragement.

"I wanted to ask you if, tomorrow . . ."

Does he even listen? Does it interest him? Does he realize that he's the head of the household and that the three of us depend on him?

Olivier takes little notice of his father and quietly organizes his own life. He often goes out in the evening, less frequently since Manuela has been with us. After dinner he goes up into his bedroom, or into the sort of laboratory that he has fixed up in the attic, and which happens to be just next to the Spanish girl's room.

My mother went into the drawing room. I followed her. She automatically switched on the television set. . . . She does so every evening, invariably, whatever the program, yet this does not prevent her from hearing the slightest noise in the house. . . .

She sews. She always has some linen to mend, or buttons to sew on. I usually sit down in front of the television set too, but the programs don't always interest me and I bury myself in a book.

"It was strange the way the storm stopped so suddenly. . . ."

She looked up for a moment, as though to make sure that my words had no hidden implication. Then she simply murmured: "Yes. . . ."

There was a clatter of plates in the kitchen, where Manuela was washing up. I knew that as soon as the maid went upstairs my mother would get up, muttering: "I must make sure she's switched off . . ."

But her real purpose would not be to see to the electric light or the gas stove. Some red wine had been left over and she would drink it from the bottle, with an anxious glance toward the door, for she's always afraid of being caught. When she's in this state she will drink anything, whatever comes to hand, and her cheeks gradually begin to flush and her eyes to glitter.

I am sorry for her and at the same time I resent having to pity my mother. Sometimes I feel sorry for my father too. Which of them began it?

We were babies once, my brother and I, myself first, for I am the older, I am twenty-one, and then Olivier, who is nineteen.

Did our parents behave like most other parents? Did they exchange kisses and loving words as they stood by our cradle?

It seems unthinkable. As far back as I can remember the house has always been just the same, orderly and silent, the days broken only by gloomy mealtimes.

I'm not sure that they hate one another. My father is patient, and I realize that it's not always easy. I can understand why he has taken refuge in that study where he spends most of his evenings. But surely Mother might have expected something more than patience from him?

At times I wish they would have a regular family scene, a really violent one with shouts and tears and then a temporary reconciliation.

I'm a bad judge. I am not good-looking either. I am rather plain, like my mother, though I have a rounded thick nose instead of a long pointed one in two sections.

What was the good of thinking about such things? I read; I tried to read, and from time to time I watched my mother's face. Outside the rain was dripping slowly.

The program changed to a noisy Western, and I got up to turn down the volume. Are there many families like ours living in and around Paris?

At ten o'clock my mother took off her glasses and picked up her sewing, her scissors and spools. She had not been into the kitchen as I'd expected.

"Good night, Laure. . . ."

She stood quite still for a moment while I kissed her lightly on both cheeks. And now she would go through the kitchen on her way upstairs. At last I'd be able to switch off the television and read in peace.

Does my father wait until she is in bed before going up himself? I never see them go up together. There's usually a gap of a quarter of an hour, as if they wanted to avoid any sort of intimacy, even though they sleep in the same bed.

I went on reading. Then the study door opened. My father crossed the hall and stood in the doorway, looking around him with a completely expressionless face.

"Has your mother gone up?"

I glanced at the clock on the mantelpiece. "Just over ten minutes ago."

"Did she say anything?"

I looked at him in some surprise.

"No." What might she have said? About what?

"Has Olivier been down?"

"No."

"Is he in his room?"

"In his room or in the attic, I'm not sure. . . ."

"Good night, Laure. . . ."

He moved toward me, and he too duly received a kiss on both cheeks.

"Good night, Papa."

It always seems odd to call him Papa. It doesn't go with his physical appearance, his grave, dignified bearing. He never smiles, or rather, when he tries to smile it's a mechanical twitch of the lips, with no gaiety in it.

"Aren't you going to bed?"

"Soon. . . ."

"Don't forget to turn out the lights. . . ."

As if at twenty-one I was incapable of switching off the light behind me!

"Good night. . . ."

"Good night. . . ."

But that night, the night of November 9th-10th, was not to be a very good one.

After reading for an hour or so I went to my own room and undressed. I kept thinking about the Professor, and about Gilles, who must surely feel puzzled and resentful.

Professor Czimek is not handsome. He is fifty-two, and he has a daughter of fifteen and a merry, dumpy little wife whom he married after he had left Czechoslovakia. He's one of the most intelligent men there are. But from Gilles Ropart's point of view . . .

There are times when I would rather not think, but just let myself go on living. Apparently when I was quite a small girl and my father or mother disturbed me, I used to say with a sigh:

"Can't I be let live?"

I might say as much now. I brushed my teeth, took off the slight make-up I allow myself, and, after lifting my heavy breasts with a certain pleasure, I slipped on my pajamas and got into bed.

I always find it hard to get to sleep. Thoughts and images of every sort flood into my mind, from all periods of my life. I have tried sleeping pills; I used to drop off more rapidly but would wake up after an hour or two and find it harder to fall asleep again, so that next morning I felt muddle-headed.

I suppose I have inherited my mother's keen sense of hearing. In any case, our house, although built in the last century, is as resonant as a drum.

I could hear the water dripping from the roof and from time to time a car passing along the road.

Why do I always have the impression that other people are really living and that I am not? Those cars were going somewhere, coming from somewhere. At this time of night there were people at theaters and restaurants, and some of them were laughing. Like Manuela. She's the only one who laughs in our house, regardless of the atmosphere around her. She's my age, she's beautiful, full of health and vitality. Her gaiety seems almost defiant.

I knew what I was expecting and it happened, inevitably. My brother got up in the next room. I could hear his bed creaking. So he must be undressed.

Had he waited long enough? Were Father and Mother asleep? He opened his door cautiously and crept up the stairs. Although he made as little noise as possible I heard him, and Manuela must have heard him too, for she opened her door before he had time to knock.

This was the tenth time it had happened. It had been going on for about a month; I was conscious of them standing there, above my head, embracing one another. Then I hard Manuela's throaty laugh.

Was my mother listening too? And if so, what was she thinking? My brother is nineteen, and it's natural to be in love at that age.

None the less I suspect her of being bitterly resentful; for it was happening in her own house, in her own realm, and what's more with her maid.

We have never been able to keep a servant longer than six months, and Mother treats the Spanish girl more harshly than her predecessors. Manuela seems not to notice. She goes about fearlessly singing and laughing. And for the past month she has readily admitted the son of the house into her bedroom.

They were both in bed now, apparently oblivious of the fact that they were directly above my head. I could hear everything. But at the same time I was listening, as it were, to the silence in my parents' room.

If *they* were awake they must be hearing it too.

And then a door opened slowly, their door. Then it closed again, and someone, barefooted, started up the stairs. I could even swear that I heard my father's heavy breathing. I was sure it was he. He took an endless time climbing up to the second-floor landing, where he stopped motionless.

Had he only just discovered that Olivier visited the maid in her bedroom? Or, having guessed it, was he looking for a proof?

Up in the attic the lovers carried on unsuspectingly.

My father, Captain Le Cloanec, a man of fifty-two, who always seems overburdened by his responsibilities, was standing there barefoot in the darkness, listening to his son and the maid making love.

I had suspected this, but I had refused to believe it: my father was in love, in love with Manuela, which I found inconceivable. He was so much in love as to leave his bed, where my mother might be lying awake, or might wake at any moment, to go and keep watch.

Keep watch for what? He knew now, didn't he? He needed no further proof.

Would he humiliate himself by opening the door and surprising the lovers?

He stood there motionless, torturing himself. I don't know if he really has a bad heart. When anything upsets him he sometimes lays a hand on his chest. Was he doing that now?

I had never imagined him in that situation, or in such a state of mind. I was distressed by it; I was anxious, too, on account of my mother. He stood there a long time, and when at last he came downstairs he went into the bathroom as though to give himself an alibi.

I expected to hear him and my mother speaking, but no noise came from their room. He must have groped his way back to bed in the darkness, and if Mother was awake she must have pretended to be asleep.

I had no idea what time it was. My thoughts were becoming confused and I was in a wretched state of mind. I considered getting up to take a sleeping tablet and then, without realizing it, I dropped off to sleep.

In any case, when I opened my eyes daylight was showing through the slats of the Venetian blinds, and when I drew these up I was surprised to find that the sun was shining. The road was still wet, covered with twigs and even quite sizable branches. There were drops of water hanging from the telephone wires and slipping off one by one. In our front garden a broken branch was lying by the gate.

Downstairs, Manuela was singing. Mother must have

been still in her room. She has nothing in the morning except a cup of coffee, which is taken to her in bed, and she seldom comes down until we have all three left the house.

I went to the bathroom. The door was locked.

"That you, Laure?"

My brother's voice.

"I'll be through in a couple of minutes."

I was a little late. It was past eight o'clock. However, I don't start work at the Broussais hospital until nine, and on my motorbike the trip only takes me twenty minutes.

My father was probably in the dining room, drinking his tea and eating toast and jam. We scarcely ever breakfast together, but each of us comes down at his own time.

"Just look at that sunshine! If anyone had told us yesterday . . ."

"Yes. . . ."

I heard Olivier getting out of the bath and taking down his bathrobe.

"Half a sec. . . . I'll let you in. . . ."

The door opened. His hair was standing on end and his face was still wet.

He frowned as he looked at me. "What's the matter with you?"

"I didn't sleep well."

"Don't tell me you have sick headaches too!"

He has no patience with Mother.

"I've got to talk to you, Olivier."

"When?"

"Now. . . . As soon as Father has left. . . ."

For my father goes into Paris by a motorbike, too, so that Mother can use the car. He only takes it when the weather is bad, as it was yesterday.

"What did you want to talk to me about?"

"Wait. . . . I'll go down and have breakfast with you. . . ."

I had on my yellow dressing gown. I combed my hair a little and brushed my teeth while my brother went into his room to dress. He takes no care of his clothes and they always look as if he has slept in them.

We heard Father's motorbike starting up and then the gate creaked. He almost always opens it in the morning and shuts it at night.

"Are you coming?"

"In a minute. . . . You go down and ask Manuela to do me a couple of fried eggs. . . . With sausages, if she's got any. . . ."

Manuela, serene and smiling, at peace with the world and with herself, called out cheerfully: "Bonjour, mademoiselle. . . ."

On her lips, the words became: "Z'ou, made-zelle. . . ."

She has not been in Paris more than a year. She has had two jobs already. She's got a friend whom I once saw waiting for her on the road, a tiny dark creature called Pilar.

"Morning, Manuela. I'd like a big cup of coffee and two pieces of buttered toast. My brother's just coming down, and he'd like eggs and sausages, if you've got them. . . ."

She seemed to be laughing. Everything amuses her, even trying to understand what one says to her in a foreign language. She's not much taller than her friend Pilar but plumper, and full of vitality. She moves as gracefully as if she were dancing. She's Andalusian, from a village called Villaviciosa, in the Sierra Morena, somewhere to the north of Cordova.

She had gone back to the kitchen by the time my brother appeared, with his hair still wet.

"What did you want to say to me?"

"Sit down. We've got plenty of time. . . ."

It was Saturday. "Have you got classes?"

"Only lab work. . . ."

Olivier, who is studying chemistry, goes to classes at the Faculty of Science in the former Halle aux Vins. His dream is to have a big noisy motorcycle, which my father refuses to buy for him.

"Every school kid has a motorbike. . . . I look ridiculous on mine, with my long legs. . . ."

I am very fond of him. He's a nice boy, but he's moody. He'll flare up over the least thing and insult me savagely, and then come to say he's sorry.

He must have guessed that I wanted to talk about Manuela, and he was curiously and vaguely uneasy. I waited until we had been served. He smiled at the

17

Spanish girl with a tenderness that I had not expected from him. When my parents are not there he can show his real feelings.

I had thought it was only a passing fancy, a purely physical passion, but that single glance of his had shown me something else, while Manuela herself grew a little graver.

"Morning, Manuela. . . ."

"Morning, Monsieur Olivier. . . ."

She pronounced it "Olié," and it sounded very sweet and tender. She went off swinging her hips, and closed the door. The dining room smelled of coffee and fried eggs and sausages, but it was also pervaded by the same odor as all the rest of the house, that musty smell of damp wood and hay that you often get in the country.

"Well, what is it?" my brother said impatiently.

I picked my words carefully for fear he would fly into a rage, particularly as one could never be sure that Mother was not behind the door. She lives in slippers, her everlasting red slippers, and she goes about noiselessly.

"You ought to be careful, Olivier."

He flushed, and retorted with defiance in his voice: "Careful about what?"

"Last night, something happened while you were up there. . . ."

"Mother?" He was on edge already.

"No. . . . Father. . . ."

"What did Father do?"

"I suppose I'd better tell you. . . . You're old enough to . . ."

"What did he do?"

"Some time after you'd gone up he came out of his room in his bare feet and went upstairs too."

"What for? To listen at the door? To look through the keyhole, maybe?"

"I don't think so, Olivier. He stood on the landing for a long time and I think he was distressed."

"What d'you mean?"

And as I did not answer immediately Olivier pushed his plate aside and stood up suddenly.

"You're not going to tell me that he's . . . that he . . . that . . ."

He could not bear to utter the words.

"Yes."

"Oh, that would be the end! As if it weren't bad enough to have a crazy mother!"

"Hush. . . ."

Olivier is pitiless. He treats Mother harshly, especially when she has been drinking, and he makes no allowances for her. He has several times admitted to me that he wanted to leave the house, to drop everything and take a room in Paris, even if he had to work his way through college.

"There are plenty of people at the University who earn their living."

He was striding up and down the room, trying to contain himself.

"What business is it of his if Manuela and I are in love?"

He turned to glance at a photograph of my father as a young man, a junior officer with a faint mustache.

"What was he doing at my age? . . . Unless he's always been as lifeless as he is now, which wouldn't surprise me . . . A solemn . . . a solemn . . ."

He seemed reluctant to speak the word, but it broke out in spite of him:

"A solemn imbecile!"

"Take it easy, Olivier."

"It's obvious you're not the one involved. Does he worry about what you do at Broussais?"

At this I blushed myself, and did not press the point. It's true that it isn't easy to get at my father's real personality. I myself sometimes dismiss him as a second-rater, trying to maintain a lofty image of himself.

He spent the war years in Algeria, in an office job, and he likes to imply that he was in the secret service. Now, with the rank of Captain but in civilian dress, he works in an office on the Boulevard Brune, somewhere near the Jean-Noël stadium, so that he is only a few hundred yards from the Broussais hospital. It's an old building that used to be a private house and now belongs to the War Ministry. The official name of his department is "Bureau of Statistics." According to Father, his work is top secret and involves confidential information about counter-espionage.

I learned the truth one day from a young doctor at Broussais.

"I've got an uncle in that place too. They're the people who send the money to our agents abroad. They've got roundabout ways of sending it so that it can't be traced. . . ."

In short, my father is a sort of accountant or cashier.

My brother stopped walking about and stood in front of me.

"What d'you want me to do?"

"I don't know. I only wanted to warn you."

"Do you admit that he's ridiculous?"

"I pity him."

"And because he's to be pitied, I've got to be miserable?"

"I didn't say that, Olivier. You might perhaps see her somewhere else."

"On Wednesdays, then, since that's her only day off?"

I didn't know the answer. It was not my problem. I could not help being uneasy and unhappy about my father.

I'd been quite right to think that Mother might not be far away. She opened the door slowly; she was in her housecoat too, with her everlasting red slippers, her hair still disheveled, her face rather puffy. She looked at each of us in turn.

"Aren't you eating?" she asked Olivier, for he had barely touched his eggs and they were congealing on the plate.

"I'm not hungry."

He was unnecessarily curt. He added, as though reluctantly:

"Good morning, Mamma."

"Good morning."

The greeting did for both of us. She seemed not to notice me. She opened the door and called out: "Some more coffee, Manuela."

She must have been eager for us to go so as to drink some red wine, unless there is a bottle of brandy or whisky in the house. When she is on one of her bouts, anything will do.

She sat down, weary and listless, and Olivier announced:

"It's time I went."

This was not true, but I could understand his wanting to leave. I finished my breakfast and wondered, yet again, whether there were other families like ours.

"What's going on?" She wanted to make me talk.

"I don't know. Why?"

"I heard him shout."

"He often talks like that."

She knew I was lying. She didn't care. She looked at me with those hard, small, unhappy eyes of hers. Manuela, bursting with vitality, brought in her coffee and the contrast between the two women was almost tragic.

"Are you working all day today?"

On Saturdays I sometimes come home at noon. At

other times I am on duty all day. When I know that the Professor is going to be there I arrange to stay over.

"Did you see your father?"

"No. He'd gone downstairs when I got up and by the time I came down he'd gone off on his bike."

Why did she ask me that? Her remarks are never casual. Everything she says has a purpose, sometimes so well camouflaged that it takes some time to discover it.

"I'm sorry, but I must get ready, I'll be late. . . ."

I took a quick shower, for it would have taken too long to clean the tub and run the water. I put on the brown tweed suit I had bought for autumn, although I'm not sure whether it suits my coloring. I can't wear navy blue all year round.

When I opened the dining-room door again, Mother was no longer there. Nor was she in the kitchen, where Manuela was singing a Spanish folk song. I suppose she had gone down into the cellar.

I left by the back door and went to fetch my bike from the shed where the car is kept too. The trees were still dripping, after three days' torrential rain. Nature seemed to be slowly convalescing, and the sun was still pale. On the road I had to ride through puddles every time I met a car.

Our house is at Givry-les-Etangs, at the edge of a wood. It's a sort of villa of faded bricks with colored ceramic ornaments and a complicated roof with two pinnacles. It was built toward the end of the last century by an uncle of my father's, another Le Cloanec, who had been a colonial official in Madagascar and then in Gabon.

After a while he had resigned from the service and become a lumber merchant. This had enabled him, in a few years, to amass a small fortune and build himself this house at Givry-les-Etangs. There are in fact two ponds not far from here, the Etang-Vieux, the old pond, which has become a kind of marsh, and the Grand-Etang, the big pond, on which we keep an old boat that is always full of stagnant water.

Another villa, farther off, has been unoccupied for some years. There's a third, which belongs to the Rorives, a retired dairy owner and his wife.

There was some story about a Negress. . . . For my uncle brought a magnificent Negress back from Africa with him, and I'm not sure he did not intend to marry her. I don't know what she looked like, for there are no pictures of her, only a photograph of my uncle, a self-important paunchy figure in a tropical helmet.

She may have met someone in her wanderings around Paris. At all events, she failed to come home one fine evening, and it seems that she was later seen in a brothel where she was employed.

I learned this story through snatches of conversation overheard when one or the other of my mother's sisters came to visit her and they gossiped in monotonous voices like a running tap.

My father inherited the house, which is called Les Glaïeuls, and only a modest sum of money, since his uncle had invested in an annuity.

After Givry-les-Etangs I still have a couple of miles to ride before reaching the Saint-Cloud–Versailles road, where the traffic is heavier and I have to be careful.

Past that point I feel as if I had severed all links with home and belonged solely to the Broussais hospital.

Professor Czimek is at the head of the Immunology Department, which includes several laboratories. There are at least twenty girls working there under the direction of Mlle Neef, a spinster of fifty-five who has devoted her life to the Professor.

She cannot endure me, for she knows, even though she has never caught us unawares, that my devotion is not as Platonic as her own.

I believe everyone is aware of the situation, even though in public my relations with Stephen are those of a young lab assistant with her chief. I even avoid, during the day, looking him in the eyes, for fear of betraying myself.

Poor Ropart must have been the first to find out, since for over a year I used to go out with him and spend an hour or two in his rooms on the Rue de l'Eperon. He's an intelligent fellow, with a future. The Professor thinks very highly of him and entrusts him with important research. Did I ever think that I might someday marry Gilles Ropart? I'm not sure, but the idea must have crossed my mind, if only when the atmosphere at home became intolerable, which frequently happens.

I always knew I was not in love with him but with the Professor. I always thought of Gilles rather as a good friend, even though we had a more intimate relationship to which I did not attach great importance. As soon as I began to work at Broussais I fell in love with Czimek, but for a long time I thought him beyond my reach.

Some of the girls make fun of him, because he has retained a strong foreign accent and he is apt to make jokes one can't always understand. And he sometimes talks to himself.

He isn't at all like the conventional idea of the big chief. He isn't solemn, like my father, and his highly mobile face is rather like that of an elderly schoolboy who loves playing jokes.

None the less he's a member of the Academy of Medicine and he's been mentioned as a possible Nobel Prize winner.

I always arranged to stay on with him in the evenings when he stopped late to dissect one of our animals, a rat, a hamster, or more recently a dog. We've got more than thirty dogs in the basement, and the patients in the various hospital wards complain of hearing them howl much of the night.

Czimek carries on his work undeterred by anything, convinced that he is on the right track and that his discoveries will be of capital importance to mankind.

"What's the matter, child?"

He calls all the lab girls "child"; this makes things easier for him, for he has no memory for names, particularly French names.

"Nothing's the matter, monsieur. I just wondered if I couldn't help you."

"Help me, eh?"

He said this ironically, as if he had seen through me.

"You don't seem in a great hurry to get home in the evenings."

"I feel more at home here."

"You do! And that tall redhead, Ropart, isn't that his name? Have you stopped going out with him?"

I was scarlet with embarrassment and didn't know where to look.

I don't think he was doing it on purpose. Nor do I believe he is cynical. On the contrary; later on, I decided that it was out of a sort of shyness that he spoke like that, as though making fun of himself.

Could he have been jealous of Ropart?

"Have you been quarreling?"

"No. We were just good friends."

"And not now?"

"I never see him except here."

"Doesn't he resent that?"

"Surely not. He understood."

He went to wash his hands, very carefully, like a surgeon, and muttered a few words in his own language. He seemed vexed. He prowled about tidying up his instruments, then at last he put his hands on my shoulders.

"In love?"

There was an unfamiliar huskiness about his voice.

"Yes," I said, looking him straight in the eyes.

"You know I'm married?"

"Yes."

"That I've a daughter who's nearly your age?"

"She's only fourteen."

"I see you know all about me."

I knew, too, that he lived in a big apartment on the Place Denfert-Rochereau, opposite the Lion of Belfort.

"What are you hoping for?"

"Nothing."

"That's about all I can give you. In my position, a liaison is out of the question."

"I know."

Did he sense my fervor, my devotion, the quality of my love? I was no infatuated schoolgirl, but a woman. Apart from Ropart, I had had a couple of ephemeral affairs.

"You're a funny girl."

Then he put his arms around me and kissed me with a touch of tenderness, first on the cheeks and then on the lips.

We have never been alone together in a real room. We have never made love in a bed, except the cot that is kept for anyone on night duty.

During the day he treats me exactly as he treats all the others, with an almost fatherly and somewhat absent-minded kindliness.

I have sometimes thought that human beings don't greatly interest him. He sacrifices his time and his health in trying to cure them, to improve their lot, but as individuals they don't exist for him.

I have often wondered what he is like at home, in his family or with close friends, if he has any. He gets on well with the other heads of departments, particularly the cardiologist, but I don't think this could be described as friendship.

As for me, I belong to him. He has grown used to it. He sometimes goes a whole week without taking notice of me, knowing that I am there, that I shall always be there, whatever he may do.

I shall be an old maid. The prospect does not distress me, and perhaps someday, much later, when Mlle Neef retires, I may take her place in the department.

I think I am happy. I should be, if it weren't for our life at home, about which I would rather not think. I hate myself for feeling nothing but a sort of latent pity for my mother. As for my father, I am sorry for him too, though I resent his being the sort of man he is. If he had reacted from the first, instead of bowing his head in meek silence, might not my mother have been different? At the office, he may perhaps take people in. He takes himself in, at all events. He puts on an important solemn air, as Olivier says, but don't the people who work with him make fun of him behind his back?

He is fairly tall and broad-shouldered; he has an erect soldierly bearing, but there's a certain lack of weight and substance about him.

I wonder if other girls of my age criticize their parents. At home, we all spy on one another. Nothing escapes us, not an attitude, not a word, a fugitive gleam in someone's eyes.

"What's the matter with you?"

"Nothing, Mamma."

Father, on the other hand, does not ask questions; he just frowns, with those bushy eyebrows of his. There are tufts of grayish hair in his ears too.

"You ought to get them cut," I told him one day when I almost felt close to him.

He merely looked at me as if I had said the silliest thing imaginable. How could a man like himself, with his responsibilities, be expected to bother about the hair sprouting in his ears?

And now he was in love with Manuela and had become his own son's rival!

I couldn't bear to think of it. I settled down to work, as usual, in the smallest lab. At that time of day, on Saturdays, the Professor was giving a lecture and his assistant, Dr. Bernard, was in charge of the department.

Here, too, I feel myself spied on. Over the past year the news of my relations with the Professor has had time to spread. Do they wonder how I can have managed to attract him, plain as I am? Or do they think I'm a good match for him, with his elderly clown's face? I have heard that comment made several times. It's true that he has a furrowed, extremely mobile face and can grin as broadly as a circus clown.

What other whispers can be going around about us? I get no privilege, no promotion. On the contrary, it seems a point of honor with Czimek to give me the most unpleasant jobs to do. It's his way of replying to gossip.

"You're not usually so late. It's a quarter past nine."

"I know. My mother wasn't well this morning and the road was bad."

"Are you on duty this afternoon?"

"I don't know."

One of the dogs has just died, and it was supposed to live several days longer. "He" will certainly want to know what happened.

And in that case I would stay. I'd eat in the cafeteria, which I quite enjoy. Olivier would be going out with his friends. Only Father would have no excuse for not returning to Les Glaïeuls, but he makes a point of shutting himself up in his study and pretending to work.

The fact is that we all avoid my mother. Each of us has another life to turn to outside the house, other pleasures, other preoccupations.

She has none. Her only outlet is to take the car to do her shopping at Givry-les-Etangs and once or twice a week at the Versailles supermarket.

She has four sisters and one brother. Her brother, Fabien, manager of the Poulard chocolate factory, lives in Versailles with his wife and two children. One sister, Blandine, lives in Paris, on the Rue d'Alésia, where her husband runs a furniture-moving and trucking business. As for Iris, who is unmarried, she has a small apartment on the Place Saint-Georges and earns her living as a stenographer.

Alberte, whom we call the "fat one," is the wife of a wealthy Strasbourg grocer, and Marion lives in Toulon.

On one of our dining-room walls there hangs a photograph of my mother and her sisters as children, with their father the General in uniform, and his wife.

At one time we often had visits from one or another of my aunts, but these have become increasingly rare. I hardly know my cousins; some of them, at Toulon, I have never seen in my life.

I went on working, with my thoughts elsewhere; I was wearing my white lab coat and cap. There are about twenty of us coming and going, bending over test tubes, looking after small animals to which we have given names.

When the midday bell rang, I felt as if I had only just begun my day's work. I washed my hands, ran a comb through my hair, and followed most of my companions to the cafeteria. The nurses from the other departments were there, but they paid no attention to us, for we are a separate community.

Somebody was saying that Professor Czimek needed horses for a particular serum and wanted to turn one of the garages into a stable. To the nurses, as to their patients, the dogs were bad enough! "And now we're to have horses in the hospital. . . ."

It may or may not be true. There are always rumors going round, particularly about my boss. Nobody questions his great ability, but he's considered an eccentric who would willingly sacrifice three quarters of the hospital to his own researches.

My father and mother must now be sitting tête-à-tête in the gloomy dining room of Les Glaïeuls. Would she say anything to him? Had she been awake when he went upstairs to the second floor and stood waiting for so long, barefoot, on the landing?

I don't expect her to refer to it, except in so subtle a way as to arouse his anxiety without telling him for certain whether she knows.

Olivier must be lunching at the university cafeteria, as he does nearly every Saturday. Does he talk to his friends about Manuela? Does he feel the need to confide in them, or does he keep his love a secret?

I went on eating, watching people's faces, thinking, and ended by not being sure what I was thinking about.

2

That evening, November 10th, my father surprised me by not retiring to his study after dinner but settling down in the drawing room, which is divided from the dining room by a wide opening with no door.

I wondered whether this was in order to watch Manuela, later on, putting away dishes and glasses in the sideboard. As for Mother, she just stared fixedly at him. She was on the second day of her novena and had drunk rather more than the day before. She had begun to walk unsteadily. She would go on drinking more heavily every day until at last, still complaining of her headache, she would retire to bed for two or three days.

I had been mistaken about my father's motives. There was a prewar film on television, with slick photography and arty lighting. The men wore short tight-fitting jackets and sleek hair, the women long dresses and romantic make-up. The whole film was foolishly sentimental, and yet my father watched it with interest, probably with nostalgia. I had the impression that he had seen it long before, perhaps when he was about twenty or perhaps later, at the time of his marriage. I was surprised to see him staring so attentively at the screen, and it seemed to me, at some points, that his eyes were dimmed with tears.

I went up to bed first, for I had not slept much the night before. I don't know if they talked to one another in my absence; I presume not.

During the night I was wakened by Olivier's motorbike roaring around the house, then by footsteps on the gravel. My brother must have been drunk—I gathered that immediately—for his hand fumbled for quite a while before thrusting the key into the lock. Then he went upstairs with loud, noisy steps, clinging to the banister.

Without pausing on the first floor he went up to knock at Manuela's door, which she opened to him.

My parents, who sleep more lightly than I do, could not have failed to hear; but this time Father did not go upstairs. Over my head, I don't know what they were doing but I could hear the sound of footsteps, furniture being pulled about, and my brother's voice raised in anger.

At last I heard him fling himself upon the bed and, after a while, the Spanish girl joined him there.

There was a lull. A quarter of an hour later somebody went into the bathroom, my brother presumably, and I heard the water being flushed repeatedly.

I did not hear him come downstairs; eventually I dropped off to sleep again. Did he spend the night in the maid's attic? Did he go back to his own room? He was being so noisy and clumsy that in that case I think I would have heard him.

Was this not a sort of challenge, a declaration of war? He took no precaution against being heard, quite the contrary.

Next morning, at half past nine, Manuela left the house before anyone else to go to Mass at Givry. Sunday is not her day off; she takes Wednesdays so as to go out with her friend, who works on Avenue Paul-Doumer, near the Trocadéro.

Rain was falling gently, a thin steady rain that must have been cold. I watched Manuela walking down the road under her umbrella. She never misses Mass and she always makes the sign of the cross before meals.

My father finished his breakfast and went into the hall to get his hat and raincoat. He goes to Mass too. He is a Breton from Pouliguen, near La Baule, where his father used to keep a small bookshop and where his mother still lives in an old people's home.

My brother and I have been baptized. I went to first Communion, but my brother never did, I don't know why.

My mother's family are not Catholics, and the General was said to have been a Freemason; I can't say whether this is true or not.

Olivier came down in shirt sleeves and slippers, his hair all on end and his shirt unbuttoned. His eyes were swollen, his face was tired, with red blotches, and, looking at him closely, I noticed the mark of a bite at the back of his neck, below his ear.

"Has he gone?"

"He went to church in the car."

"Much good may it do him. And Mother?"

"Manuela took up her coffee before she went out."

"Has she gone on foot?"

"You'll find coffee in the kitchen. The pan's all ready for your eggs. Would you like me to cook them?"

"I'm not hungry."

His expression of disgust told the whole story. He had a hangover, and his head must have been aching.

"Were you with friends?"

"When?"

"Last night, when you were drinking."

"I went on drinking by myself mostly, after they'd gone."

"Don't you think you ought to be careful, Olivier?"

He glared at me aggressively.

"So you're on their side too?"

"No, but I feel it's pointless to . . ."

"I've the right to live, haven't I? D'you call it living, the way they exist, the way we all exist in this house? If they're crazy it's not my fault."

I poured him a second cup of coffee and he sugared it mechanically.

"I'm fed up," he growled. "If only I had some money I'd go off with Manuela. She's the only thing that keeps me here. And now my idiotic father has to start running after her with his tongue hanging out. He's making a real fool of himself! If he only knew how he revolts her. . . ."

I don't know why I felt a pang. Olivier's brutal words shocked me and made me think of my father with compassion rather than disgust.

And yet I can understand my brother's bitterness. I, too, sometimes revolt against our life at home, and I keep wondering whether there are many other families like ours.

What went wrong? Or have things always been like this? Were my father and mother never in love, were they never a proper couple, or did it all happen later, after we were born?

I incline to lay the blame on Mother, who must always have been somewhat unbalanced. Was there ever a suggestion of treatment? Did she agree to see a psychiatrist? She has always been somehow out of gear with reality, sometimes so subtly that only members of the family could notice it.

Was my father the right man to take on responsibility for her? Had he done all that he might? I blame him, too. Then I feel sorry for him. I am sorry for all of us, in fact, and if I could not escape to Broussais every morning I think I'd go crazy too.

Olivier asked me: "Are you going out this afternoon?"

"I certainly am."

Sundays are deadly at Les Glaïeuls. It's difficult to escape from one another. After lunch, sometimes, we all go up to our own rooms and try to sleep. I don't know about the rest, but that's what I do and I sometimes doze for part of the afternoon. When I go down into the drawing room I almost always find my mother watching television and knitting or sewing. Father is in his study, reading newspapers and magazines.

As for Olivier, he makes a point of being out and he seldom comes home for supper on Sundays.

Just now, he was smoking his first cigarette and exhaling the smoke with a defiant air. He had the fierce look of a man in love, ready to challenge the whole world. He glanced at the clock, probably thinking that Mass must be nearly over; Manuela would take a good twenty minutes to walk back from Givry. It was still raining; the sky was hung with low gray clouds, motionless, with darker patches.

"I'm going to take a shower."

"It'll make you feel better."

He looked at me irritably.

"So I don't look too good? If you want to know, I got tight on purpose. I was with Marcel Pitet. We had a few drinks and then he wanted to go home. When I was by myself I went into the first bar I came to and drank several brandies at the bar. A woman tried to pick me up and I ended by offering her a drink and telling her all about it. I needed to talk to somebody. I said: 'That bastard my father . . .' And she offered to console me. At one point I vented my rage on her, perhaps because she made the mistake of saying: 'You can always get another girl!' I must have made a scene. The barman paid himself out of my wallet and then gave it back to me and pushed me into the street."

"Go and take your shower."

"That's all you can say, is it? Have some coffee, some strong black coffee, go and take a shower. And when you come down again try to keep calm and don't make a scene."

I had had enough of him. I went into my own room and looked out at the trees, where the yellow leaves that had not yet fallen glistened in the rain.

I sometimes lay the blame for it all on our house, on those perpetually dark woods, on the ponds, the Etang-Vieux and the Grand-Etang, on this godforsaken place where we have no neighbors but that ridiculous couple the Rorives. Not only do they naïvely display their satisfaction at having made good, after thirty years in their dairy on the Rue de Turenne, but they feel obliged, because they're our neighbors, to call on us from time to time. They seem to have noticed nothing. They invariably bring a cake or some chocolates. They smile as if we had welcomed them with open arms, and they both go and settle in the drawing room.

"Hasn't the heat been trying!" Or the damp. Or the drought. Rorive spends hours fishing in the Grand-Etang, where he sometimes catches a tench. One day when he had caught two fine ones he brought them to us, wrapped up in leaves. "To take away the taste of mud, you must clean out the insides with a little vinegar."

My mother is often alone when they come, and if my father is there and catches sight of them in time he hastily retreats to his study.

And yet it's the Rorives who are normal, surely? I turned to look down the wet road and I saw our car coming nearer. Father was driving and there was someone beside him; I could not make out who, but I guessed immediately. When the car came nearer I recognized Manuela's face.

It seemed natural enough. They had both been to church; it was raining. The church was a long way off. My father, being alone in his car, had offered the girl a lift home. . . .

It might be natural for other people, but not in our family, and I hoped that neither my mother nor Olivier was looking out of the window.

The car skirted the house. I heard the car door slam, then the sound of two people's footsteps on the gravel, and Manuela's voice saying something I could not catch.

She's a cheerful creature, the only one in the house; on Sundays as on every other day she goes about looking pertly seductive, with her black uniform stretched tight over breasts and hips.

I often wonder if she does it on purpose, if it's her way of provoking my mother, perhaps my father too. No, her mocking glances are particularly directed at my mother.

Olivier came into my room without knocking while I was still dressing.

"Did you see?"

"What?"

"Father brought her home."

"It's raining."

"That's no reason for picking her up in the car and making up to her. I must ask Manuela if he didn't try to put his hand on her knee."

"Olivier, you're exaggerating. . . ."

"You think so? You obviously don't know anything about men, apart from your old Professor. . . ."

"Let me finish dressing, will you?"

He was venting his rage on me now, forgetting that he would have known nothing about my private life if I hadn't confided in him one evening when I felt the need to tell someone about my feelings.

"A madhouse, that's what it is!"

He went out, slamming the door behind him. At half past twelve, when lunch was served—our usual Sunday chicken—we met once more around the table, each in his usual place. Manuela went back and forth from the kitchen, bringing in the dishes.

No one spoke. No one felt like speaking. Olivier, very flushed, poured himself three glasses of wine in quick succession, and Father pretended not to notice. Mother, however, was watching his every movement and expression.

One word, one gesture would be enough to start a row, and I felt that my brother was finding it hard to restrain his urge to unleash it. This might have relieved him, but it would make life more difficult for all of us subsequently.

Olivier left the table first, after tossing down one more glass of wine. Ten minutes later we were still in the drawing room drinking our coffee when we heard his bike and, looking through the window, saw him ride past.

It was my turn to escape next, and I went upstairs to put on my boots and get my raincoat.

"I expect I'll be back for dinner," I said, half opening the drawing-room door.

The two of them were left together; they could not escape. Their only resource was to stay each in his own little world, my mother in the drawing room, my father in his study. The bad weather would not even allow them to go for separate walks in the wood or around the ponds. Perhaps the Rorives would call, bringing a tart or a cake, to tell how when they kept the dairy they used to do their marketing in the Halles at three o'clock in the morning. He did the buying, and she cooked the various vegetables which were subsequently set out on the white marble table, since many customers in those days bought their vegetables ready cooked to save time.

I made my way to the Champs-Elysées, where, in spite of the rain, there were queues in front of the movie theaters. Didn't this mean that other people, even couples, even families, felt the need to kill time and escape from their everyday routine?

I had no date with any friend, not even with a colleague, for I have no real girl friend. My interests are different from those of the other girls. Many of them have a boy friend with whom they go out on their free days. Others get together in twos and threes and go for picnics in the summer.

Some of them, to be sure, would be among those waiting for their turn in front of a theater door.

And I waited too, wondering what the Professor does on Sundays. Perhaps he, too, goes out with his wife and daughter. They have a small country house in the neighborhood of Dreux, but this was no time of year to be staying there.

Do they entertain friends? Are they gay and cheerful? I should have liked to know all about him, but there are aspects of his life that are still hidden from me.

On his desk there is a photograph of his wife and daughter in a silver frame. His wife, in my opinion, is rather ordinary-looking; as for his daughter, who wears her hair long, she has a precociously grave look in her eyes.

What can those two say to one another? What can a father and daughter talk about? I was reduced to imagining their dialogues, for my father and I have never had any real conversations, except of a purely practical nature.

"You're sure you are doing your best?" Father would say to me while I was still at school. "You're not afraid of failing your finals?"

Then, when I told him I wanted to become a lab assistant:

"That is one of the finest professions for a woman, provided you have the vocation for it. Above all, it requires patience."

As if he knew! As if he'd tried out everything in his life, whereas he has always worn blinkers and sees only what he wants to see!

I found a seat at the end of a row and, like the rest of the audience, I stared at the screen where people who were in love with each other had to overcome all kinds of obstacles; at the end, needless to say, they won.

Was that what the hundreds of people sitting in the darkness of the theater had come to seek?

After the movies I went for a walk in the Champs-Elysées, looking at the shop windows. The rain had stopped. Suddenly a dense crowd had poured onto the sidewalks.

I went into a cafeteria on the Rue de Berry for my

dinner. When, plate in one hand and glass in the other, I looked for somewhere to sit, I found myself facing a very young girl, who couldn't have been over sixteen. Her face was distorted with distress and bewilderment. All the time I sat there she was holding back her tears, and she averted her face in embarrassment whenever I looked at her.

My brother must have come back very late. I did not hear him.

Monday, November 12th: the date is marked with a cross in my diary. That means that Stephen asked me to stay on in the evening and that we made love on the cot in the little yellow spare room.

It's only in my thoughts that I call him by his Christian name. Otherwise, even in our most intimate moments, he's still the Professor and I call him *monsieur*, as we do all the heads of departments: an emphatic *monsieur*, with a capital *M*, so to speak.

He always looks at me with curiosity, as though he didn't quite understand me.

"Are you satisfied with your life?"

He must have noticed my hesitation. "Don't be afraid to tell me frankly."

"Here, in your department, I'm very happy."

"And elsewhere?"

"At home, life is different. I often feel I'm stifled there."

"Are they strict?"

"It's not that. Everyone's always watching everyone else. I catch myself spying on the others too."

"Don't you want to have a home of your own, and children?"

Looking him squarely in the face, I replied categorically: "No."

"Is your mother unhappy?"

"My father is, too."

His mobile face is marked with fine deep lines. When he talks to me like that he suddenly appears to me in a different light, like a father persuading his daughter to confide in him. My own father has never sought my confidence. He merely stares at me in astonishment, as though he could not understand my attitude.

There was a certain irony in the Professor's voice as he said to me:

"In short, you want to remain a spinster?"

He does not believe it. He thinks that someday I shall meet someone who attracts me and that then I shall do what they all do. He cannot know that I might have married Gilles Ropart and that it was on his account that I did not.

I suddenly began to think about my aunt Iris and her lonely existence in an apartment on the Place Saint-Georges. She works for a big advertising firm on the Avenue des Champs-Elysées.

She was the mistress of her boss, who was young and daring and successful in everything he attempted, treating life as though it were a juggling act. He had married very young and lived separated from his wife. He was the typical Parisian *élégant,* always in the public eye and able to have any woman he wanted.

Was my aunt jealous or was she satisfied with her share in him, knowing that he would always come back to her?

One afternoon he died suddenly, as though struck by lightning, while he was passing through one of the offices. He was forty-two.

My aunt is all alone now. She must be about forty herself. She's not even a real widow, and she still works for the same firm, although it is now under entirely different management.

She's the most attractive of my aunts, who have all been given pretentious names: Alberte, Iris, Blandine, Marion. The only son, who runs the Poulard chocolate works, is called Fabien. Was this a fancy of the General's, or his wife's?

I should have liked to be in touch with her, to visit her sometimes on the Place Saint-Georges, where I have never set foot. I think we might understand one another. She is the youngest of the Picot daughters, and she comes once or twice a year, driving her small yellow car, to visit us.

My mother is not fond of her. I don't think she is fond of any of her sisters, which is why I scarcely know my relatives. The others see one another, even Alberte when she comes from Strasbourg to Paris, and Marion, the naval officer's wife who lives at Toulon.

Has my aunt Iris been happy? Is she happy now? I passed her on the street the other day. She did not see me and I did not dare run after her. She has grown much thinner, and this gives her features a certain hardness that reminds me of my mother.

"You're a funny girl, Laure."

It seldom happens that he calls me by my first name. His little eyes were, as usual, sparkling with mischief; you never know if he is laughing at you. I believe he was not laughing at me but that he was somewhat touched.

"Well, we shall see what the future has in store for you. . . ."

My mother went on drinking, and by Monday evening she smelled not of wine but of brandy or whisky. As there was none in the house I suppose she had driven into Givry or Versailles to buy a few bottles.

On such occasions she always gets up later. On Tuesday morning I came down early, expecting to be the first. I went into the kitchen and caught my father unawares; I couldn't swear to it, but I am almost sure he was passing a note to Manuela. In any case she quickly slipped a folded piece of paper into her bodice.

"I'd like some marmalade today," he said to maintain his composure.

Poor man! At his age, to be reduced to such childish subterfuges!

I poured my coffee and announced that I did not want any toast; I was not hungry. However, I sat down in the dining room opposite my father.

"The wind is from the west," he said. "We'll have some more rain."

I said yes and went on looking at him as he bent over

his plate. I think of him as an old man, and it seems ludicrous that he should be in love. And yet he's only about a year older than the Professor. So I'm vexed with myself for being unjust, but I cannot help it.

My brother came down just as I was going out to get my bike. When I returned home for lunch, my mother's eyes were ringed with red and she went about like a sleepwalker. I don't know why I came home for lunch instead of eating in the cafeteria. My father usually lunches near his office and Olivier goes to the student restaurant.

I seemed to be trying, unsuccessfully, to make contact with my family. Just as for a long time I tried to find out where my mother hid her bottles. Father hunted too, I know, with no success. She is more cunning than all the rest of us.

In the evening I went to my English lesson, an advanced class that I attend twice a week.

And on Wednesday, as usual, Manuela stayed in bed late. It's her great delight every Wednesday. She does not necessarily sleep; she lies smoking cigarettes and reading Spanish novels. When she hears no more noise from the ground floor she comes down in her nightdress and dressing gown and makes herself a great bowl of milky coffee.

I am sure she relishes every moment of her morning, and she doesn't go out until midday, in her Sunday best, to catch the bus at Givry. As a rule she lunches in a restaurant with her friend Pilar, who works for a rich industrialist on the Avenue Paul-Doumer.

Then they go window-shopping together, have dinner somewhere or other, and end the evening at a dance hall on the Avenue des Ternes, called Chez Hernandez.

She generally comes back on the last bus that drops her at Givry at twenty minutes after midnight.

This Wednesday my father came home rather later than usual; it was past eight o'clock, and we were waiting for him to sit down to supper.

Mother had not bothered to cook anything. She had opened a can of soup and bought some cold cuts. She even served bottled mayonnaise, which a few years ago she would never have tolerated in her house. She was really unwell. Obviously her drinking bout must be nearing its end, for she could not go on much longer like this.

When we heard the car in the garden, she remarked in a voice she could scarcely control: "Well, so he's come back after all!"

Olivier and I stared at one another, and I felt that my brother, despite his resentment against Father, was deeply shocked. It was not until we were at table that I noticed my father's face. When he came into the room he had merely greeted us casually. Was I mistaken? I could have sworn that a faint perfume hung about his face or clothes, and his mouth had a bruised look, as though from long and passionate kissing.

And in his eyes there was an almost impish sparkle. I had never seen such an expression on his face. He seemed to have lost his stiffness and much of his solemnity.

So long as Olivier . . .

I watched my brother; he, too, was sniffing the air, with a tense frown.

"So we didn't have any rain after all. . . ."

Father's remark met with no response. Nobody echoed it. Mother looked at him with a vicious expression. It was one of the most miserable meals we had ever had. Only Father seemed not to notice. His shining eyes told of his inward exultation. He ate hungrily, resigned to silence since nobody would answer him, but jubilant none the less.

Had he in fact been passing a note to Manuela in the kitchen that morning? Most likely; and it was likely, too, that he had been proposing a rendezvous. I'm sure of nothing, but in our family we are accustomed to interpreting signs.

He had been with her. It must have been the Spanish girl's perfume that still hung about him and that my brother was trying to identify. As for my mother, if she said nothing she was none the less carrying on an inward conversation with herself, and several times she gave a sarcastic smile.

After folding his napkin, my father made for his study and I felt that Olivier was on the point of following him. I stared at him as though to hypnotize him, saying to myself: "He must not go in there. . . ."

He did not go in. He stopped in front of the door.

I whispered as I went past him: "By and by, in my room . . ."

Then I started clearing away, as I do every Wednesday. Mother made a show of helping me, then swayed and clung to a chair for support. I led her to her armchair, murmuring: "Another of your dizzy spells . . ."

Was she taken in? I switched on the television and escaped into the kitchen, where I began washing the dishes. I didn't know whom I was angrier with, Manuela or Father.

When I went up to my room I found Olivier stretched out on my bed. He had not bothered to take off his shoes and he had flung his jacket across the room, aiming at a chair but missing it.

"What d'you want?" he asked, aggressively.

"I want to have a chat with you."

"What about?"

"You know very well. You've got to calm down, Olivier. You can't go on living in such a state of tension."

"So I look tense, do I?"

Lying there on my bed, indeed, he seemed calm enough, disturbingly calm.

"You mustn't take this business too seriously."

"Are you referring to that old swine?"

So he had reached the same conclusions as myself. At least, that was what I thought at the time.

"Is that how you speak of Father?"

"I'd like to know how you'd speak of him if you were in my place. I saw them."

"What do you mean?"

"I'm telling you the plain truth. I'd suspected something. Yesterday I noticed them making signs to each other, like accomplices, and she asked me not to go up and see her."

"How did you happen to meet them?"

"I didn't meet them. I followed Manuela. I knew where she usually meets her friend, at a restaurant on the Avenue Wagram. A little before one o'clock Manuela went in. On most other Wednesdays they spend the afternoon visiting shops, or at the movies.

"They left the restaurant at about two and walked toward the Etoile. There they parted, both in very high spirits, and Manuela went down into the métro.

"I had my bike and I couldn't follow her. I had a sort of inspiration. I rode as fast as I could to the Porte d'Orléans métro station, the nearest to Father's office. He was there, waiting on the sidewalk, looking at his watch from time to time."

"Did he see you?"

"No, I don't think so. In any case, I don't care if he saw me or not. She came up from the station and they exchanged a few words before going off toward the Avenue Général-Leclerc."

He got up, feeling restless.

"D'you understand now? He was as fidgety as a boy and he kept stroking her arm. They stopped in front of a small hotel. Father looked embarrassed. He leaned over her and talked in a low voice."

"Did they go in?"

"Yes."

"You went away?"

"You don't suppose I was going to stop there on the sidewalk while less than thirty yards away they were up to their filthy tricks? Just wait till she comes home. As for him, he can afford to wait."

"He's your father, Olivier."

He brought home to me the absurdity of my remark. "Was that why he went to bed with my girl?"

He was furious; he was fuming with rage. I was terrified that he might go down and create a scene.

"Are you really fond of her?"

"Yes."

"Even now that you've seen what . . ."

"Even now!"

He was ruthless, threatening.

"You ought to face up to things. You know it can't lead to anything."

"So love has got to lead up to something, has it? And d'you think your affair with your Professor is going to lead up to anything?"

I was stupefied. "So you know?"

"I've known for a long time. More than six months."

"Who told you?"

"I happened to be going out, for a short while, with a girl who's a nurse at Broussais. She asked me if I was your brother. She put on an air of mystery that intrigued me and I bombarded her with questions until she told me the truth."

"What's her name?"

"Valérie Saint. She's in the Cardiology Department.

Her boss and yours are great friends and sometimes work together."

"I know."

"You see why I was expecting you to defend him." He meant Father.

I did not know what to say. I did not even know what to think.

"I assure you, Olivier, it's not the same thing at all."

"Yes, it is!"

"How can you say that?"

"You're forgetting that you dropped another fellow for his sake—a young intern whose name I've forgotten."

He even knew about my affair with Gilles Ropart.

"Those old men are all swine and the girls that run after them are tarts."

"Olivier!"

"Well, so what, Olivier?"

I burst into tears. I couldn't help it. Last time my brother had seen me crying I had still been a little girl. It upset him, and he muttered: "I'm sorry."

He was striding about the room, his hands behind his back, and in the study just below Father must have heard the sound of his footsteps, the echo of our excited voices.

Olivier added: "You're a free agent. You can do what you like with your life."

"At any rate try to keep Mother out of all this."

"If you think she doesn't know as much as you do!"

"What makes you believe that?"

"Do you suppose Father can have left his bed and gone up to the second floor to listen to us through the door without her noticing? And this evening, drunk though she was, she must have seen from his face that he hadn't come straight from the office. The fool didn't even realize about the scent."

"How is it that she's never said anything?"

"She never says anything. She notices. She's biding her time."

"Do you think she'll want a divorce?"

"No."

"What else can she do?"

"She can throw Manuela out, for one thing, and then I'll find the money somehow to follow her, even if I have to steal it."

I dried my eyes. My head was throbbing and I went to open the window to cool it.

"Anyhow, now you know. . . . And don't you worry about me. . . . I'm not a kid. . . ."

He's just nineteen. It's true that I myself am only two years older.

"Good night, Olivier."

"Good night, Laure. Try to sleep. Take a sleeping pill."

"Thanks. You, too."

I had a feeling that he was reluctant to leave me, that there was suddenly a new bond between us. At last he opened the door and went up into the attic he has turned into a laboratory.

I hadn't the courage to go down and find my mother

sitting alone in front of the television set. That evening, I didn't want to see any of them again. I'd done my best. It was not my fault if I had not succeeded.

I took one tablet, then another, to make sure of sleeping. I got ready for bed, lay down, and switched off the light.

I must have slept for quite a while, two or three hours or even more, and then I was wakened by the sound of gay voices outside the gate; some young men were joking very loudly in Spanish.

Manuela had not returned by the last bus. It was not the first time this had happened. She had found some friends to bring her home and they all seemed in high spirits, probably rather tipsy.

They went on shouting jokes at her until she had reached the front-door steps and then they drove off noisily.

Had my brother gone down? I turned on the light for a moment to see the time. It was twenty-five minutes past two. I tried to go to sleep again but involuntarily I kept listening. In Manuela's room I could hear two people's footsteps, and soon I recognized Olivier's voice, literally screaming. A chair fell over onto the floor. Someone collapsed heavily onto the iron bed.

My parents could not fail to have heard. Would Father dare go upstairs to intervene? Manuela uttered a single cry. My brother went on abusing her, then suddenly his voice broke. He seemed to be begging her pardon, beseeching her.

Then she spoke to him in a gentle, plaintive tone and without realizing it I dropped off to sleep again.

3

I expected a catastrophe, of what sort I did not know. It might be the dramatic departure of Olivier, who has no professional training and who, left to himself, would certainly not go on with his studies.

I did not for a moment think that my father and Manuela might leave the house together, and I am convinced that this was my mother's opinion too.

In any case, it seemed to me impossible that the situation should grow any tenser without leading to an explosion.

On Thursday morning Olivier came down from the top floor with no attempt at concealment. On the contrary, he stopped to light a cigarette, taking his time, as though he wished to assert the rights he had acquired.

He had shaved and was fully dressed. He had evidently spent the night in the maid's room and had bathed in her bathroom.

He was looking tired but calm, somewhat too calm. Father was still at the table when Olivier entered the dining room, and the two men exchanged no greeting but pretended to ignore one another.

Was it deliberately that when the Spanish girl brought his coffee and eggs my brother patted her behind with a proprietary air?

My mother was at the end of her tether. The shaking of her hands was painful to watch and she had developed nervous tics, the sudden twitching of certain muscles that distorted her face for a moment and revealed the extent of her deterioration.

She had almost stopped eating, and she was sick every day. It happened to her once on the staircase before she had time to reach the bathroom.

In theory, her novena should be nearing its end, but there was no sign of any decrease in her consumption of alcohol; quite the contrary. We would see her grinning to herself, sometimes with a glance at us, as if to say: "You're not so clever, the three of you! You imagine I don't know, but I really know more than any of you!"

I cannot say when she first took to drinking. I never

dared raise the subject with my father, for it's more or less taboo in our house. I have often tried to remember what she was like during my childhood. I can recall her looking melancholy, often depressed and unhappy. I would ask her: "Are you crying, Mamma?"

"Don't pay any attention to that. Grownups are unhappy about things that children can't understand."

I suppose that when she was like that she had already begun one of her drinking bouts. They were much less frequent in those days. Her brother, her sisters, and her brothers-in-law still used to visit us. Our boy and girl cousins used to come on Sundays and play with us in the garden.

In the afternoon we used to go for a walk around the ponds, the children in front of the grownups. How old was I? At least five, for my brother had already learned to walk.

This went on for two or three years. Then my mother quarreled with one of her sisters, the one who married a furniture mover.

Then the same thing happened with her brother.

Iris, my only unmarried aunt, still used to come and bring us candy, and she was on good terms with my father.

From time to time Dr. Ledoux was sent for from Givry. He is still our family doctor, and although his hair is gray I cannot realize that he has grown old.

Two years ago Mother had a particularly bad drinking bout which ended in a prolonged fainting spell. Her pulse rate was barely forty-eight per minute and her lips were bluish. The doctor came immediately and gave her an injection even before carrying her to bed with Father's help.

I followed them. It was the first time I had heard the two men discussing the subject.

"I'll come back and see her tomorrow. She's going to sleep deeply."

"There's no danger?"

"Not for the present."

"And later on?"

"If she begins drinking more and more frequently, and more and more heavily . . ."

"Is there nothing to be done?"

"In theory, yes. I could send her to a nursing home for a sedation cure. It lasts about a month. After that she'll go for several weeks or months without drinking. But there are ninety-nine chances out of a hundred that she'll start again.

"What's needed is to find out the precise cause of her behavior. . . ."

I remember my father saying gravely: "When she was only a child, her brother and sisters used to tell her that she was ugly and would never find a husband."

"You see she did find one."

I thought I saw a rather bitter smile on my father's lips.

"She's always been rather withdrawn. Because of her looks, she tended to avoid boys and girls of her own age."

"Had she begun to drink when you married her?"

"I couldn't swear to it. If she was drinking, it was so moderately that I never noticed. At first she wanted to do without a maid and insisted on doing all the housework herself. I suppose marriage must have been a disappointment to her."

"But the children . . ."

"She was a very good mother while they were small and depended on her. After that she seemed to acquire a certain indifference. I would not say she lost interest in them, but . . ."

My father made a vague gesture instead of finishing his sentence. It was the first time I had been treated as an adult and allowed to listen to such a conversation, and it was doubtless at that moment that I felt closest to my father.

"She feels ashamed. After she has spent two or three days in bed, taking nothing but vegetable broth, she wanders timidly about the house like a ghost, with a look of melancholy resignation on her face.

"She sticks to the legend she has created: 'Why do I have to endure these dreadful headaches?' "

Mother is wearing herself out, as Dr. Ledoux had warned us. She is aging fast, and like my father she sometimes presses her hand to her chest.

She often irritates me. I bear her a grudge for not having given me a childhood like other people's, and even now for continually jeopardizing the harmony of the family. But what sort of harmony is it, and what sort of family? We are all at odds with one another. The two men are not on speaking terms, won't even look at each other.

All the same, I'm sorry for my mother. I pity her. I am confusedly aware that she is not responsible and that she suffers more than we do.

The last time Dr. Ledoux was sent for he suggested that she should be examined by a psychiatrist.

"It's worth trying. But when she hears the word she'll probably dig in her heels and declare that she's not crazy. In the broad sense of the word, that's true enough. All the same . . . I'm not a specialist. . . ."

"What do you advise me to do?"

"I don't know, I'll frankly admit it. The cure might be worse than the disease. A psychiatrist would want to have her under observation in a hospital. . . ."

"She'd never consent to that."

"Well, as long as the family can stand it . . ."

Thursday passed. In the evening I found the remains of a coffeecake in the kitchen. I knew at once that my aunt Blandine must have come to visit Mother, for she invariably brings a coffeecake.

There is no longer any open disagreement between my mother and her sisters, even though they seldom see one another. They tend, rather, to blame my father nowadays.

"A proud, surly man, who thinks of nothing but his profession and never says a kind word to his wife."

Did he ever take her to the theater or to dine in a

restaurant, like other husbands? Did they ever travel abroad together?

She was the only one of the sisters who had never left France, who did not know Spain or Italy. We had once spent the holidays on the Riviera, and that was all.

My aunts made no secret of their opinion in front of me. Their brother, Fabien, was even harsher. He would have liked to be considered the protector of the family.

"I cannot understand how you can go on living with a man like that. I never understood why you married him, anyway, but at that time Father was still alive and it was no business of mine. . . ."

My mother would sigh. She had gradually got used to playing the part of a victim. I sometimes wonder if she has not acquired a taste for it.

As for Aunt Blandine, she's a big woman with a ringing voice and almost mannish gestures. When she married Buffin, he was a rough, decent fellow who had just bought his third truck and drove one of the three himself.

Now he has about twenty, some of them traveling daily to Lyons and Marseilles, not to mention four or five moving vans with his name in big black letters against a yellow background.

My aunt has become as vulgar as Arthur, her husband, who is fairly coarse-spoken. One of their sons is already in the family business, while the other, who is said to be brilliant, is studying medicine and plans to go to the United States for a term next year.

I had known General Picot, my grandfather, a tall lean man who impressed me with his elegance and breeding. His wife, too, is a person of some refinement; since she became a widow six years ago, she has lived alone in a small apartment in Versailles, quite close to her son's home.

For twenty years the General dragged his family about from one town to another, as he was posted to various garrisons. The brother and sisters were now scattered and we ourselves lived in that gloomy house, Les Glaïeuls, because an uncle of my father's had taken it into his head to bequeath it to him.

I sometimes feel that the house is to blame for everything, and that my mother's moods are due to the atmosphere in which she lives all day long.

There's something depressing about the mere smell of damp, the sight of the dripping trees, particularly the two big pine trees.

Friday came, and I was surprised that nothing had happened. On Thursday the Professor kept me late, but he was preoccupied, anxious to know the result of his current experiment. He had inoculated several animals, some mice and a couple of dogs, and was watching them day by day in the smallest of the laboratories, at the far end. The assistants worked in relays, day and night, noting the animals' behavior hour by hour, their temperature, and their blood pressure.

He would trust nobody else with the blood analysis, which he attended to himself. I did not know exactly what he was looking for. He never spoke of it, but one could guess from his nervous tension and the occasional gleam in his eyes that if everything went off satisfactorily he would have made an important discovery.

At midday on Friday Gilles Ropart sat down beside me in the cafeteria. We had kept on very good terms. I suppose that like myself he has pleasant memories of our period of intimacy.

"I've got a great piece of news to tell you, Laure."

He had always called me *vous* in front of people and now he had no occasion to say *tu*.

"You're going to get married?"

"Correct. At least, I've been engaged since yesterday."

"Someone from Broussais?"

"No, someone who's got nothing whatever to do with medicine."

"Do I know her?"

"No. Her father's an architect and she's a student at the Beaux-Arts."

"Have you known her long?"

"Six weeks. Love at first sight, in fact."

He was making fun of himself. He was an odd fellow, very gay, with an enormous sense of humor.

"One of these days I'll introduce her to you."

"Have you told her about us?"

"I haven't dotted the i's, but she's guessed that I'm no virgin."

He laughed, and looked me straight in the eyes, reflectively.

"And you?"

"What about me?"

"Still the same great love, the same total devotion?"

"Is it ridiculous?"

"No. It's probably very fine. In any case, he's a lucky man. I just wonder what will happen in ten years, twenty years."

"I've an aunt who has lived alone for more than ten years and who's not unhappy."

"You know I nearly asked you to marry me?"

"Why didn't you?"

"Because I was sure you'd say no. Was that true?"

"Quite true."

"Why?"

"I don't know. Perhaps because I'm like those nuns who feel the need to sacrifice themselves."

"So really, what you needed was a god."

"If you like."

It strikes me as odd that life goes on, that thousands and millions of people go on living their lives outside the tense atmosphere of Les Glaïeuls.

Walking in the streets, I have always been impressed by the thought that everybody one sees is the center of his own universe and that his preoccupations loom larger than what is happening in the world around.

I am like everyone else, thinking about my mother, my father, and Olivier. I often think about myself, too, about the time when I shall be able to have an apartment in town. I can picture myself keeping house in the evening or early in the morning. I don't believe I should mind the loneliness but, on the contrary, that it would be a relief to me.

When I carry my dream to its conclusion I visualize Stephen coming there sometimes in the evening, to sit down in an armchair and chat with me while he smokes. He is a chain smoker and his fingers are stained brown with nicotine. As his hands are often busy he keeps his cigarette stuck to his lips and drops ash everywhere, even on our animals' coats.

The sun was shining, but it was rather cold. I thought about my mother, eating all by herself in the dining room at home. There were just those two women alone in the house, hating one another. That may not be quite accurate. Undoubtedly my mother feels a real hatred for the Spanish girl, who has robbed her of husband and son at once.

But Manuela? She still runs up and down the stairs humming songs from her own country, one in particular, a sort of endless carol of lament of which I have involuntarily learned snatches.

> *La Virgen se está lavando*
> *entre cortina y cortina;*
> *los cabellos son de oro,*
> *los peines de plata fina;*
> *pero mira como beben,*
> *pero mi . . .*

Then a gap in my memory. I have a feeling I've got the word-order wrong. It hasn't the least importance since I don't understand it, except perhaps for the last line:

por besa a Dios nacido.

I imagine that means: Because a God is born. On Manuela's lips this becomes a love song. One might expect her, like most other people, to break into a smile only when someone looks at her. But I have often come upon her unawares, when she has not heard me coming, and I have always found her wearing the same contented smile.

For her, life is beautiful. Everything is fine. Everything is good. She makes love with my brother every time he visits her in her room. She has made love with my father too, I'm sure of it, simply because he gave her a note asking her to meet him outside a métro station.

She must have other lovers too, at Hernandez's dance hall, where she goes every week.

I have had several lovers too, but I was not necessarily gay. On the contrary, I was quite clearheaded: I knew that I was not in love but that I wanted to prove to myself that I could attract men. It was during the period when I thought myself plain and gawky.

Gilles Ropart was the last of the series, and I believe he understood, for he always treated me affectionately.

Now I no longer wonder whether I am ugly or not. In any case, I am not really ugly nor, perhaps, physically unattractive.

True, I haven't a particularly pretty face and I dress

badly. I look my best in uniform, especially in summer, when I wear hardly anything underneath the white nylon.

My figure is good, though, my breasts especially, and most of the men I have slept with have been surprised on seeing me naked.

Did my mother once have a good figure too? There's nothing left of it. She is so thin that you can see all her bones, and she's getting bent, she walks with her shoulders hunched up as if she was afraid of being beaten.

I think about my mother too much. I feel that I'm judging her objectively and yet at the same time I am aware of subtle bonds between us. For instance, I tell myself that I might have been like her. If I had got married I don't think I would have been capable of blending with another person's life.

I am fond of children. Sometimes when I tell myself that I shall never have any I feel rather melancholy. But actually I should not have the necessary patience.

Even a child of Czimek's. I have thought of that. I nearly asked him to give me one. I should have been wrong. I can only dedicate myself to one single person, and I have dedicated myself to him once and for all.

I am not even afraid of his deserting me, and that is not because I have too high an opinion of myself. I play only a small part in his life, a diversion in the midst of his preoccupations, but he needs that diversion.

Sometimes he strokes my hair with a queer sort of smile.

"My little thing . . ."

And I think I understand what he means. I take up no room. I'm hardly noticed. I ask for nothing. But I am always there, always ready. He knows it, and he tries to understand my feeling.

There's no question of our being a couple. He is far above me, so far that I don't criticize him, I don't try to understand him.

He *is*. That's enough. And if it entered his head to make love to other lab assistants I should not resent it, I should be almost glad of it for his sake, provided he came back to me.

Do nuns criticize God, and are they jealous of other worshipers?

If I were to talk like this to other people they would probably take me for a fanatic, a hysterical creature, whereas to me it's all quite simple and quite natural. Dear Ropart is the only person who has understood.

I seldom think about myself at such length. It's not narcissism. I am a Le Cloanec, after all, and what has been going on at home for the past week affects me as much as the rest. I have been trying to see where I stand in relation to them, to decide what influences I have undergone.

Then I went back to my work in the lab. The sun was streaming through the wide bay windows, and most of the animals were dozing in their cages.

The Professor spent much of the afternoon in his room, dictating letters and notes to a secretary. It was past five o'clock when he came into the labs and he went straight into the one that interested him most at the moment, the little one at the far end.

He motioned me to follow him, as well as one of my colleagues who has a special gift for handling dogs.

"Get Joseph out."

This was a reddish-brown mongrel that had been on the premises for over six months, and which owed its nickname to a resemblance to one of the porters.

We held the dog down on one of the tables, and it was so used to this that it didn't struggle, merely looking at us each in turn as though wondering what was going to happen next.

Czimek had adjusted his stethoscope and begun to sound the animal when the door opened and there stood a stout elderly woman who works at the reception desk.

"There's a policeman who insists on seeing you, monsieur."

He did not reply, he was not listening, he merely grunted, still bending over Joseph. Framed in the doorway, I saw a tall police officer who seemed ill at ease and was very red in the face. He must have been a sergeant, for he had several gleaming stripes.

The Professor did not turn his head but took his time, and, still preoccupied with the dog, finally growled: "Another offense?"

"No, Professor. I should like to speak to you for a moment. . . ."

"Well, go ahead."

"I think it would be better . . ."

"Are you worried about these young ladies? Don't mind them. They're used to such things. . . ."

"It's about Mme Czimek. . . ."

"What has happened to my wife?"

This time he left the dog in our hands and glanced sharply up at the man, seeming surprised to see him in uniform.

"A traffic accident, monsieur . . ."

"How is she?"

"Seriously injured. . . . She's been taken to Laënnec. . . ."

The Professor seemed more stupefied than anything else. His immediate reaction was disbelief.

"You're sure it's my wife? There may be other Czimeks in Paris. . . ."

"You do live on the Place Denfert-Rochereau?"

Beads of sweat suddenly stood out on his forehead. He had eyes for nobody but the policeman, who scarcely dared speak.

"What happened?"

"She was in a taxi on the Boulevard Saint-Michel. I suppose she was on her way home from the Right Bank. . . . Suddenly a heavy truck coming from the opposite direction drove straight across the boulevard to the left. . . . We don't know yet whether the driver, for some reason or other, lost control of his vehicle or whether he was taken ill. . . . He's not in a fit state to speak. . . ."

"My wife . . ." the Professor urged.

"The driver of the taxi was killed immediately and

74

your wife, gravely injured, was taken to Laënnec Hospital. I was told to inform you. . . ."

Czimek mopped his brow and reached out for the telephone.

"Get me Laënnec, please, mademoiselle. . . . Yes, it's Professor Czimek. . . . Hurry. . . ."

We no longer existed. Nothing existed for him but the telephone by means of which he was to learn his wife's fate. She had very light blue eyes, a broad Slav face, a kind motherly smile. I thought of the photograph, with his daughter, on his desk.

"Hello! . . . Is that the intern on duty? . . . This is Czimek, at Broussais. . . . I'm told they brought my wife in a few minutes ago. . . ."

He stared mistrustfully at the telephone.

"Tell me about her condition. . . ."

The policeman turned his head away.

"What? . . . Before?"

He repeated incredulously: "Before . . . before she got there?"

His face was puckered. I averted my eyes too, because he was unconsciously weeping, his whole face distorted.

"Yes . . . Yes, I understand. . . . I'm coming immediately. . . ."

He strode through the laboratories without noticing anyone, without trying to hide his tears.

"I didn't dare tell him at once," muttered the policeman. "I wanted to prepare him."

I shed no tears, but my head was reeling and I hurried to the cloakroom to cool my forehead with a towel soaked in cold water. I wanted to . . .

Of course, I wanted to be with him, holding his hand so as to give him courage. Suddenly I was of no use, and perhaps he might even bear me a grudge?

Now that his wife was dead, he might be feeling remorse about our relations. I thought of their daughter Marthe, who was only fourteen and who was still childish and unspoiled, innocent of the powder and lipstick that most girls use.

I had been to their home just once, by chance, when the Professor had flu and was spending three days in bed. Dr. Bertrand, his chief assistant, had asked me to take a report to him and I had to wait for an answer.

The apartment house is spacious and well lighted. On the third floor I pulled a gleaming brass bell-knob, and a stout woman in an apron let me in. There were skis in the hallway, for it was winter. I don't know if the Professor goes skiing but his wife and daughter certainly did. I remember, moreover, that they used to go to Switzerland every winter and that he joined them there for a few days.

The apartment seemed cut in two by a wide hall, broader than those at Broussais, and on either side, right up to the ceiling, there were shelves crammed with books. Not the handsome bound volumes you find in libraries but books of every description, some of them very tattered. In one room, at the far end, a phonograph was playing.

I envied the inhabitants of that bright, airy apartment. Most of the doors stood open. There was nothing stiff, far less stifling, about it, as in our house. Life could go on freely there, and nobody had to walk about on tiptoe.

I had to wait for quite a while, listening to the music. Mme Czimek crossed the hall, some distance away from me, and went into the room from which the music was coming, and I heard voices, one shriller than the other but both good-humored.

Somebody brought me the answer, and I went away again. I had had no further occasion to visit the Place Denfert-Rochereau.

"You'd better go home."

"Why?"

"You're as white as a sheet. Stop in a bar first and have a glass of brandy."

Anne Blanchet was speaking to me, a tall, likable girl whom I did not know very well.

"Don't wait to have a fainting spell. Run along! I'll tell Dr. Bertrand you felt unwell."

It was true. I was overcome with dizziness, and my legs felt limp. I pulled off my lab coat and went downstairs without waiting for the elevator.

Just across the way there is a restaurant with a bar. Nobody was there but a waiter setting tables. He called out to me: "What d'you want?"

"I'd like a brandy."

Reluctantly he interrupted his work, looked at the clock, and then at the bottles set out in front of the mirror.

"The barman doesn't come till six and I'm not too sure . . ."

He picked up a bottle and showed me the label.

"Will this do?"

I nodded. I was imagining Czimek at Laënnec Hospital, on the Rue de Sèvres, in front of the probably mangled body of his wife. No doubt he would have stopped weeping. That first reaction must have been due to shock. He had just lost, as though by amputation, a major part of his life, for he was already married when I was born. His wife had also been a refugee in Paris, and was studying there.

When they came to know one another she left the University and, so he had told me, they lived in a single room in Saint-Germain-des-Prés. He had added, nostalgically, that they had been very poor and had often had nothing but bread and cheese for a meal.

"I spoke French very badly. So did my wife. And people laughed at us. Not unkindly. They laughed as if we were very comical. . . ."

I supposed that Marthe, their daughter, was at school. I wondered at what time she got out, and who would tell her the news.

Would the body be taken back to the apartment and laid out in the main bedroom? I didn't know exactly what the proceeding was and I was very upset. I so badly wanted to be by his side and to share his emotions!

"I'll have another. . . ."

The waiter looked at me in some surprise.

"That'll be eight francs. At least that's the price written on the barman's list."

I drank it at one gulp and I went out. I had no wish to go straight home, where I should be alone with my mother. I preferred to walk about in the gathering darkness. The street lamps were alight and there were lights in the shop windows too. I found myself, eventually, on the Avenue du Général-Leclerc, without knowing what streets I had been through.

"Looking for someone, darling?"

I turned my back on the man who had stopped to accost me.

I saw the door of a small hotel wedged between two shop windows. "*Hôtel Moderne.*" It was a seedy-looking place. An enamel plate announced: "Rooms to let by the month, week, or day." The door was open, and the passage leading to the office was poorly lighted.

The Professor must be holding his daughter in his arms, for he had nobody left but her and she had nobody but him. Wasn't this going to complicate their life?

I suddenly blushed. People might believe that I was hoping . . . No, no! The idea had never occurred to me, whatever might happen. . . .

I felt tired. I sat down in a café. When I reached home at last my father's motorbike was there, so I knew that I should not have to face Mother alone.

He was in the drawing room, reading his paper, and I could not resist telling him:

"My chief's wife was in an automobile accident this afternoon on the Boulevard Saint-Michel. She died while they were taking her to the hospital. . . ."

He looked at me thoughtfully. He was poles apart from Czimek, whom he had never seen and about whom I seldom spoke, just as I am poles apart from his colleagues, whose names I don't even know.

"Was she young?" he asked at last.

"About fifty, I suppose. Perhaps less. I don't know, I've only seen her from a distance. . . ."

He turned to his newspaper again. My mother was upstairs. She must have spent part of the day in bed and I could see at a glance, when she came down, that she had been drinking heavily.

My brother did not come home for dinner. There were just the three of us at table, and I tried in vain to start some kind of conversation. Nobody listened to me. I stopped talking. In my thoughts, I was at the apartment on the Place Denfert-Rochereau.

Were the two of them, father and daughter, sitting down to a meal there? They could not spend all the time watching by the dead woman's bed. Would the undertaker's men come the next day and hang the room with black draperies, patterned with silver tears?

I was not accustomed to death. I had known only my grandfather's, and then I was too young to take in details. I remember chiefly the candles and the twig of box with which people pretended to sprinkle the corpse with holy water.

For my grandfather, even if he really was a Freemason, had had religious obsequies. I vaguely remember arguments on the subject. My uncle Fabien had insisted on a Mass and an absolution, on the grounds that a secular funeral would damage our reputation; his in particular, I suppose, for Poulard's slogan was: "The family chocolate."

My mother went up to bed earlier than usual; in her present state she soon grew sleepy after dinner. As for my father, who went up soon after, I suspected him of retiring early so as to avoid meeting his son.

Olivier came home about eleven o'clock while I was still downstairs, reading an English book but paying little attention to it.

"Are they both upstairs?"

"Yes."

"I prefer to see as little of them as possible. If it was in my power, they'd never see me again. How is Manuela?"

"Just as usual."

"There hasn't been a row?"

"Not since I came back."

"What's the matter with you? You look as if you'd been crying."

"My chief's wife is dead."

"Had she been ill?"

"An accident on the Boulevard Saint-Michel."

"Young?"

Fifty, for him, was a great age. After a moment's silence he made a cynical comment:

"So now you won't need to hide."

I was afraid, on the contrary, that my small happiness was seriously threatened. I had held a modest place on the fringe of his home life and of his professional life, although I was in some degree a part of that.

But now? There was his daughter, to whom he was bound to devote much more time.

I went up to bed and wept there, while my brother openly and noisily climbed up to the second floor.

On Sunday, when I was on duty at Broussais, the Professor did not come in at all during the day, but merely looked in about ten in the evening to examine his animals.

On Monday I found myself being scrutinized more curiously than usual, and this exasperated me. I left the house early and went a roundabout way to work so as to pass through the Place Denfert-Rochereau. The shutters of two third-floor windows, the ones on the left, were closed. This was no doubt the room that had been arranged as a mortuary chapel. Had two prie-dieus been brought in, as in Grandfather's case?

I went straight to the little laboratory where Czimek did his personal research. Good old Joseph was up and about and did not seem to be in pain. He even scratched the wire guard to attract attention.

I looked after the animals as usual. At ten o'clock I heard footsteps in the main laboratory and soon I saw the Professor come in. At first he took no notice of me. His first glance went to the animals.

His face was so drawn, his eyes so tired, that he seemed to have grown thinner.

"How is it you're here?"

"It's Monday, monsieur."

He shrugged irritably and called the two lab assistants.

"Please come, mesdemoiselles." He did not ask me either to stay or to go and I stood there as though rooted to the ground.

"Put Joseph on the table for me."

I was reminded of the policeman's arrival, when he had been sounding the brown dog as he now proceeded to do.

"You see: there's no rattle in his throat, his breathing is easy, his pulse is regular. . . ."

He patted the dog's head briefly; his eyes were far away.

"Anything happened?"

"One rat died, in the second cage."

"I expected that. When Dr. Bertrand comes, ask him to do the autopsy."

He looked at me again, opened his mouth, and then decided to keep silence.

I did not lunch in the cafeteria but in a small restaurant nearby. It was a cold gray day. I tried to go for a walk, but I soon felt tired.

How would Czimek spend his time, this afternoon? His wife had been alone in Paris when he first knew her. He himself had no relatives in France. He had few acquaintances, and these were almost exclusively colleagues.

He and his daughter must be alone in that apartment

with the dead woman, apart from the maid, who would stay in the kitchen. He must be feeling hostile toward me, as I had foreseen, because he was angry with himself. It's unlikely that I shall ever regain our former relationship.

And only last Monday . . . I can't believe it.

Finally I went home to dinner. I found my father and mother watching television. A man and woman were embracing on the screen, and then the woman burst out laughing.

The stillness of the house was uncanny. I asked Father, stupidly:

"Is Olivier out?"

I had only spoken for the sake of saying something, and he answered curtly: "I've no idea."

We had dinner. Only Manuela went on smiling as if, for her, life was good in spite of everything. Afterward I watched television too, for I hadn't the heart to read. Father retired to his study.

Shortly after ten o'clock my brother came in. I imagined he would go straight up to his own room or to the second floor, but to my surprise he came into the drawing room.

He was a little tipsy. This seldom used to happen before our recent scenes. He was not a heavy drinker; he seemed to have taken to drink out of defiance.

"Have you got any liquor, Laure? You must know where Mother keeps her brandy."

She started but did not even turn to look at him.

"No, I don't know."

Turning to Mother, he demanded: "Your brandy, Mother . . ."

"I haven't any."

"Don't talk nonsense. Tell me where you hide it, so that I can treat myself to a glass or two. Tonight I want to get blind drunk."

He was drunk already, and he was talking very loud. He seemed to be spoiling for a fight, and he kept looking toward Father's study.

"Well, are you going to get me that bottle?"

"Go up to your room."

"D'you realize that you're talking to me as if I were a kid of ten?"

"Go up to your room," she repeated in a sort of panic.

He was clearly becoming more and more aggressive.

"If you think I'm going to obey a woman like you . . ."

Then the door opened and my father appeared.

"I wish you wouldn't talk so loudly."

"Perhaps *you* know where Mother hides her brandy?"

"I'd be obliged if you would hold your tongue."

"And I want to get drunk."

"Then go and do so elsewhere."

"I still belong to the family, don't I? This is where I'm supposed to be living."

"On condition you behave decently."

"Oh, so we behave decently in this house, do we? Do

you behave decently, when you take your son's girl to a filthy, disreputable hotel?"

"I must ask you to . . ."

"And I won't! I've got the right to speak, like any other human being, and I intend to do so."

My father turned to Mother. "You'd better go upstairs, Nathalie."

She stayed in her chair, listening, her eyes still fixed on the television screen.

"Manuela!" Olivier called loudly.

"She's gone upstairs," I said, hoping he would go up to join her.

It was quite true, in fact, that she had gone up and that the light was out in the kitchen. I went in, switched it on, and seized the bottle of red wine, which I took into the drawing room with a glass.

"Here you are. This is all I can find."

Father stared at me, wondering what I was up to. Olivier had reached the point where it seemed best for him to drink as fast as possible and as much as possible, so that he would have to go up to bed.

"Your health, Mamma. You treat yourself to brandy, but your son has to put up with poor red wine, like a day laborer."

"Olivier, leave your mother alone."

My father was trying to seem firm, but he failed to impress my brother, who was too far gone.

"You keep quiet! It's the best thing you can do, I promise you. You see, some things are so disgusting that a man who does them loses any right to interfere with other people. As for my poor old boozer of a mother . . ."

"I warn you that . . ."

Father took a step forward, his fists clenched.

"No, really! Don't tell me you're going to hit me! You forget that I'm stronger than you now."

"I order you to shut up and above all to leave your mother alone."

Then another voice spoke; it was my mother's, saying: "Let him speak, he's quite right. You and I are equally disgusting. . . ."

It was all so stupid and pointless. Each of them was trying to find the harshest, most wounding things to say. They were flaying one another alive.

It was scarcely more intelligent of me to threaten them: "If you don't shut up I shall turn off the lights."

And for a start, with no particular motive, I switched off the television.

"I shall decide tomorrow what steps to take," declared my father with bogus dignity, walking toward the door.

"You do that! In the meantime, take care you don't go up to the wrong landing. You might regret it, for up there you're not my father any more."

He poured himself another glass and gulped it down.

"As for you, Mamma, I think I owe you an apology. Living with a man like that must be enough to drive one to drink."

Tears were running down my mother's cheeks, and I tried to remember if I had ever seen her crying before. It seemed to me this was the first time.

"Go up now, son."

She never used to call him that. I was amazed, and so was Olivier.

"Have I hurt you?"

"Don't worry about me."

He went up to her hesitantly and furtively kissed her forehead.

"You're all right, all the same!"

And to me: "Good night, Laure."

He made his way laboriously upstairs, reached the first-floor landing, and then went on up to the attic. Mother cast a brief glance at me, but seemed at a loss as to what attitude to take.

"It's not his fault," she finally muttered.

She was obviously referring to Olivier. What did she mean, exactly? That it was not his fault if he had been drinking? That it was not his fault if he had attacked my father and, incidentally, herself? That it was not his fault if he had fallen in love with the maid?

She listened to my father's footsteps as he got undressed. She was waiting for him to be in bed, and perhaps asleep, to go up herself.

"You can go up, Laure."

I knew she would say nothing more. It was astonishing that she had spoken so much that evening. Indeed, for one moment she had seemed to me almost human.

"Good night, Mother."

I did not kiss her. I seldom do.

"Good night."

Perhaps she wanted to be left alone downstairs to have a drink.

4

I was surprised, on Tuesday morning, to see the Professor going around the labs, examining some of the animals and giving instructions as he does every day before closeting himself in his office with Dr. Bertrand.

Because a person has lost a loved one, we expect him to take no interest in anything but his grief, and yet life goes on, he eats and drinks, talks and works.

I followed him, as usual. There were three of us

going around with him, ready to note down his observations, but he seemed not to notice my presence. I was simply there, as if I were part of the background. Two or three times his eyes fell on me, because I was in his field of vision.

Could he really have aged so much in three days? He had lost his prodigious vitality, and I had the impression that the man before me was just a man like anyone else, I'm ashamed to say a man like my father. His eyes had lost their brightness, their vivacity, their habitual sparkle.

I felt I had to visit the house where the dead woman lay and I dared not go alone; I went from one to another of my colleagues trying to find one who would go there with me at midday. Some of them curtly refused. Others looked at me with an ironical smile. I finally persuaded two, one of whom, Maria, was a stout placid country girl whose parents were farmers.

We ate quickly. Maria had no means of transport, but the other girl, Martine Ruchonnet, whose father is a well-known lawyer, had a small car and drove us to the Place Denfert-Rochereau.

The shutters were still closed over two windows on the left-hand side of the third-floor apartment. The funeral was to take place the next morning and the undertaker's men had begun hanging black draperies over the door.

We went up in the elevator. We had no need to ring, for the door stood open. Once again I saw the long, wide hallway lined with books. Even the skis still stood there. A warm smell of cooking mingled with the smell of wax candles.

On the left the door of the mortuary chamber stood wide open; there were candles burning, a sprig of box, and flowers in profusion, including vases standing on the floor.

She had not yet been laid in her coffin but was lying in state, as it were, on a bed, dressed all in white, with her hands folded over a rosary.

I crossed myself, as I had seen others do. I seized the sprig of box and made the sign of the cross in the air, while I cast a glance at the nun who was praying in one corner.

Had sisters of charity been engaged to watch in turn over the body, day and night, since there were no relatives to do so?

The hands around which the rosary was entwined fascinated me. They were strong hands with square-tipped fingers, the hands of a woman still close to the soil, accustomed to doing her own housework and if need be to do a man's chores.

My mother's hands are long, with slender pointed fingers, and she makes a great fuss when she happens to break a nail.

Were the Professor and his daughter somewhere in the apartment, having a solitary meal together?

Someone came in, a working-class man in heavy shoes, who crossed himself awkwardly and stood cap in hand gazing at the dead woman.

I felt that I was in an unfamiliar world, and the impression clung to me all afternoon. I had thought myself close to the Professor. Now I realized that I knew scarcely anything about him and that I had perhaps been an unimportant digression in his life.

When I returned to Les Glaïeuls that evening it was raining again and a strong wind was blowing. I was surprised to find myself the first one home. Neither my father nor my brother was there, although it was half past seven. I looked around for my mother and did not find her either in the drawing room or in the dining room.

My instinct told me that something was happening, and when I went into the kitchen I saw there not Manuela but my mother, wearing her apron.

She looked tired but less nervous than on previous days. Could her novena be drawing to a close? She was busy putting a dish of ham and macaroni into the oven.

"Hello, Mother."

She looked at me as if she were surprised at my speaking to her.

"Hello."

"Is Manuela upstairs?"

"No."

"Where is she?"

"She's gone."

"Did you send her away?"

"She wanted to go back home."

This surprised me, but I did not pay much attention to it, for Czimek was still my main preoccupation. I should have liked to comfort him, to be of some use to him. During the afternoon it had been another girl, a tall gawky creature whom I disliked, who had taken the collection for a wreath.

"Are you sure you didn't give her the sack?"

"She left the house of her own accord."

"You didn't have a quarrel?"

"She must have made up her mind before. She came downstairs in her street clothes, carrying her suitcase, and asked me to pay her what I owed her."

Father came in presently. He, too, seemed to notice a change in the atmosphere of the house and he called up the staircase: "Nathalie!"

When he eventually came into the kitchen he dared not ask where Manuela was. Mother provided the information, with a savage irony.

"She's left!"

He seemed not to understand.

"When is she coming back?"

"She's not coming back."

I broke in, to have done with it: "She's given up the job to go back to Spain."

He said nothing but turned away, went to sit in the drawing room, and unfolded a newspaper. He had obviously had a shock. I, meanwhile, set the table so as to help my mother, but I was thinking only of the Professor and of his wife, who, that night or very early tomorrow, would be laid in her coffin. The folded hands, the rosary, the presence of a nun in the mortuary chamber had surprised me, and I wondered if Czimek was a Catholic, if he was really a believer.

In that case, had he been to confess his relations with me, which he must consider a sin? Did he bear me a grudge for having, so to speak, offered myself? For I realized that I had tempted him.

I desperately wanted him to notice me. I wanted to become his mistress. I wanted to be something more to him than an insignificant colleague.

I was sincere then, and I still am. I have dedicated my life to him and I have come to realize, today particularly, that I know practically nothing about him.

My brother came home at last. He looked tired and preoccupied. He slumped into an armchair in the drawing room, seemingly unaware of my father's presence. He, too, picked up a newspaper and lit a cigarette.

When he saw me in the dining room he called out:

"So it's you who sets the table now?"

"As you see."

"Where's Mother?"

"In the kitchen."

"And Manuela?"

"She's gone."

He leapt to his feet, grim-faced.

"What did you say?"

"I said that she'd gone."

"Did Mother throw her out?"

"She says not."

"You mean to tell me Manuela went of her own accord?"

"I don't mean to tell you anything at all. I wasn't here. I've only just come in."

He turned to glare fiercely at Father and then strode into the kitchen.

"What have you done with Manuela?"

And Mother repeated in a dull voice: "She's gone."

"What did you say to her?"

"Nothing."

"You're lying."

"Have it your own way."

"Admit that you're lying, that you forced her to leave."

"No."

It was beyond him. He rushed upstairs to the second floor, where we heard him moving about, opening and shutting drawers and the doors of the big wardrobe.

When he came down again his look was grimmer than ever, but he said nothing.

"Dinner's ready."

The soup tureen was in the center of the table. We sat down in our usual places, myself opposite Mother and Olivier opposite Father, and helped ourselves in silence.

Dinner was scarcely over when Olivier went off without a word and we soon heard the sound of his motorbike. Did he know exactly where Manuela's friend Pilar lived, on the Avenue Paul-Doumer? They must have talked about her; he may even have met her at Hernandez's, the Spanish dance hall on the Avenue des Ternes.

I cleared the table and washed the dishes. I do that whenever we are servantless, which happens quite often. Most of our maids stay two or three months, six at the most. Some of them leave after a week, unless Mother dismisses them because she considers them lacking in respect for her.

"You're being disrespectful, young woman." How often had I heard this remark during my childhood and adolescence!

On these occasions I have to get up earlier in the morning and make the coffee, and go to the gate to bring in the bottle of milk, the bread, and the newspaper.

Before leaving for Broussais I do my room and my brother's. Finally I knock at my mother's door and put a cup of coffee on her bedside table.

I don't know if other children are like me. Even as a small girl I avoided, as far as possible, going into my parents' room, because of the smell. Everyone has his particular odor, of course, but when I smelled theirs I felt I was being thrust into an unpleasant intimacy.

This is still the case, whereas Olivier's odor, for instance, does not offend me.

I was sound asleep when my bedroom door was flung open noisily and the ceiling light was turned on. It was my brother, his hair and face wet with rain. The alarm clock showed nearly midnight.

"What's happened?"

"Don't worry. Nothing that concerns you personally."

"Did you find Pilar?"

"How did you know . . ."

"It wasn't hard to guess."

"She hasn't seen Manuela. She's had no telephone call."

"Perhaps they weren't such close friends after all?"

"Apparently they were. They told one another everything. Pilar knew about my father."

"What sort of girl is she?"

"A skinny little dark creature who always seems to be making fun of people."

"Was she making fun of you?"

" 'If Manuela's really gone,' she told me, 'you'll have to find someone else.' "

"Did she add that she'd be willing to take her friend's place?"

"Yes. I went to the airport, because she'd come from Spain by air. They sent me from one ticket counter to another and in the end they told me that they weren't allowed to give any information about passengers.

"At the Gare d'Austerlitz, where I went next, there's such a crowd that the reservation clerks can't remember whom they've sold tickets to.

"Do *you* believe she's gone home?"

"I don't know. I was as surprised as you were when I got home and didn't see her."

"I'm convinced she's still in Paris. I expected at least to find a note from her in my room or in hers."

"D'you think she's capable of writing one in French?"

My objection impressed and comforted him.

"She'll surely find a way to give me news of herself. D'you know what I eventually did? I thought to myself that she didn't know any hotels in Paris and I went into the one to which Father had taken her. They don't remember her there. Her name's not in their visitors' book.

"Who knows? Perhaps Father has set her up somewhere so as to keep her for himself."

And my brother concluded with a single word: "Swine!"

I found it hard to get to sleep again. At half past six the alarm woke me, almost an hour earlier than usual. I went down and turned on the gas. The rain had stopped, but the sky was still gray and the heavy clouds seemed to be skimming the rooftops.

I went to get the milk, the bread, the paper. I emptied the ashtrays mechanically and tidied up a little, without really cleaning the house. Then I spread the tablecloth and set the table.

It seemed pointless to advertise for a maid. The few who answer are invariably the sort of women who can never stay in one place. Presently, no doubt, my mother would call up the agency, where they know her well.

Even if the house were not gloomy, even if my mother did not have her drinking bouts, it would be difficult to find someone satisfactory because of our remoteness from Paris. Manuela had been a sort of miracle. It was unlikely to repeat itself.

"Do you want sausages with your eggs?"

My brother turned an absent gaze on me and

repeated as if the word had no meaning for him: "Sausages?"

He said it with such a comical air that I could not help laughing.

"Just as you like, I'm not hungry."

None the less he ate the two eggs and the sausages I brought him, and he had not quite finished when Father came down. The two men deliberately ignored one another and did not even exchange a nod.

As soon as they had left I washed up the pan, the plates and cups, and folded the tablecloth, which I put away in a drawer with the napkins: all familiar actions which I performed whenever we lost a maid. Then I took a steaming cup of coffee to my mother's bedroom. I knocked but went in without waiting for her to answer. She was lying with her eyes open, staring at the ceiling.

"Have they gone?"

"Didn't you hear Olivier's bike and Father's car?"

For he had taken the car today, even though it was not raining.

She replied: "Yes. I'd forgotten."

It was unreal. She seemed to be living in a sort of dream.

"They hate me, don't they?"

It was easier to say nothing.

"It's not that girl, it's me they're angry with."

She seldom talks to me so much, and it embarrassed me. Above all, I did not want to hear her secrets.

"I give you my word, Laure, I didn't put her out. Do you believe me?"

I gave a vague nod.

"Do you hate me too?"

"I don't hate you."

I was on the point of adding: "I pity you."

It was useless. I backed toward the door while she drank a mouthful of coffee between two puffs at a cigarette. She seemed better than on the previous days. Her eyes had lost their puffiness, her cheeks their red patches.

"Even so, you'd rather have had a different sort of mother."

"I wish you were in better health."

"My health has never been good. Later, you'll understand. You're too young."

"It's time I went."

"Yes. You go."

I suddenly realized that she would be left alone in the house. It had already happened, between maids, but for no precise reason it frightened me this time. From the landing I looked at her, sitting up in bed, thin and sharp-featured, smoking her cigarette, with her cup of coffee in her hand. She was looking out of the window, and it was impossible to guess at her thoughts.

I went first to Broussais, where there was an unfamiliar feeling in the air. Everyone kept glancing at the big electric clock, and Dr. Bertrand was in a greater hurry than usual to finish visiting the animals in the three labs. He took some notes and, disregarding the clock, consulted his watch.

Only three girls, the last three to arrive, were left on duty, which was a minimum. Even Mlle Neef went, at half past nine, to take off her cap and her lab coat and put on a coat with a sable collar and a small black hat I had never seen her wearing.

A quarter of an hour later we all met outside the house on the Place Denfert-Rochereau, where a number of other people were waiting. Besides the inhabitants of the apartment house, the tradesmen, and a few neighbors, I recognized most of the big chiefs of Broussais, some of them accompanied by their wives.

Those who had not already been up, yesterday or the day before, to pay their last respects to the dead woman went up to the third floor now. I was not among them. I could imagine the Professor standing by the door of the mortuary chamber, clasping people's hands without noticing them, while his daughter and the maid were weeping in some far corner of the apartment.

The hearse arrived, followed by several black cars which lined up beside the sidewalk, with a police officer directing the proceedings.

The men brought down the coffin, then went back to fetch the flowers and wreaths; these covered the hearse completely and some of them had to be put into one of the cars.

Czimek came down; he seemed to have shrunk, and to be unaware of what was going on around him. He stared at the crowd on the sidewalk, as though he were going to thank them for being there.

I suddenly saw him as a slight, almost insignificant figure. For one moment, before he got into a car with two of his Broussais colleagues, our eyes met and I wondered if he had recognized me. Perhaps he had, but it was all over in a flash.

I wanted so much to be a help to him, to be needed! I made myself very small. I moved away and mingled with the onlookers at the back of the crowd, then I went to get my motorbike and made my way to the Montrouge church.

There, too, I stayed in the background. Most of my colleagues were gathered in groups.

Was it the organ music or the sound of the funeral procession moving up the central aisle that brought tears to my eyes? I did not even know why I was crying. I was not thinking about the woman with the short square hands, lying in her white-satin-lined coffin, nor even, directly, about the Professor, who was standing alone in front, to the right of the bier.

I heard the tinkle of the choirboy's bell and the voice of the officiating priest, who wore a great white cross on his black chasuble.

It all seemed unreal to me, I had a sense of wasteful chaos. I did not try to clarify my thought. Why did I suddenly picture my mother, as I had seen her in bed that morning, with her cigarette and her cup of coffee, staring so strangely through the window at the black trees in the garden?

She was unhappy. She made us unhappy, maybe, but she was the first to suffer from it. And my brother and my father suffered too. They had become mutually estranged and actually seemed to hate one another.

Was it possible? Would our family ever behave like a real family?

This morning, in front of the house where his dead wife had lain, Czimek scarcely recognized me, whereas my whole existence depends on him. I have no right, I am well aware of it. From now on he would devote himself to his daughter, and become more passionately absorbed than ever in his work.

I blew my nose and wiped my eyes. I was ashamed of weeping from self-pity, for indeed it was for myself that I was weeping.

I did not recognize him immediately. I was leaving the hospital and making my way toward the parking place when he emerged from the shadows. He gave me the impression of being inordinately tall, with very long arms and very long legs.

"Did I frighten you?"

It was Olivier, who hardly ever comes to meet me after my work, unless we have planned to go somewhere in town. My first thought was that he must have some bad news to tell me.

"What's the matter, Olivier?"

"I want to have a talk with you somewhere else than in that damned house. You must know some quiet little café."

"There's one just across the street."

This was the place where I had had two glasses of brandy on the afternoon of Mme Czimek's death, and it was odd that circumstances should bring me back there on the day of her funeral.

The walls were painted beige and paneled halfway up with dark wood. The room was lighted with small lamps, with imitation-parchment shades, standing on the tables. This time the barman was there.

"What'll you have?"

"A coffee. I'm tired."

"One coffee and one Scotch," he ordered.

It always surprises me to see him drinking, for it's not so long since he was a child.

"I cut my lectures this afternoon. I wanted to think things out."

He was looking at me gravely. He was quite sober; this was his first drink.

"I think I've made up my mind."

He was frowning as he looked at me. "Have you got a cold?"

"Are you asking that because of my voice or because my nose is red?"

"You haven't got your usual face."

"I've been crying."

"Because of what's happening at home?"

"Today was the funeral of my chief's wife."

He was unmoved by this. He was thinking only of what concerned him personally. But wasn't this the case with me, too?

"You said you'd made up your mind. To do what?"

"To leave home."

For some time past I had been expecting this to happen someday, but it came as a shock all the same.

"What about your studies?"

I asked this halfheartedly, just to say something.

"You know, if I went to the University it was chiefly because Father wanted it. As for chemistry, I was crazy about it when I was fourteen or fifteen; I used to make some sort of bomb that I exploded in the woods. It was just a game. Since I've been really studying it I don't see where it's going to lead me."

There is only two years' difference between us, and yet I feel so much older than he is! Is it because he's a boy? Has he remained particularly young for his age?

I felt as if an overgrown child was before me, talking about the vital decisions he had to make.

"I can't stand them any longer, don't you see? Especially now, after what they've both done to me."

I understood what he meant. My father had taken Manuela to a shady hotel and Mother had undoubtedly thrown her out. He could forgive neither of them.

"I sometimes wonder whether Mother ought not to be in a mental home. As for the man who claims to be my father, he's nothing but a depraved imbecile."

He lit another cigarette from the one he was still smoking.

"How will you earn your living? Have you any idea?"

"Not yet. To give myself time to think about that,

I'm going to anticipate my army call-up. Or even to enlist, if necessary."

"Won't you need Father's consent?"

"Do you think he won't give it with the greatest eagerness? He'll be only too pleased to get rid of me. Then he'll be quite free to run after the maids."

It was painful to find him so bitter and yet so boyish.

"I think you're wrong, Olivier. I'm sure that he's ashamed of what has occurred. It can happen at his age as well as at yours!"

"Don't defend him, please!"

"I'm giving you my opinion, and I'm asking you not to let your feelings run away with you. Wait a few days. Don't forget that your future depends on it. When you've finished your military service, you still won't have a job."

"I'll manage somehow. I'm not afraid of roughing it. At least I shall be my own master."

He drank a mouthful of whisky and retched.

"Besides, if I stayed at home I'd start drinking. It runs in the family. There! Now you know what's in my mind. Don't you understand?"

"I understand, but I beg you to wait a little, say a week."

"That's a long time!"

"Not in relation to one's whole life."

"Well now, what sort of life have our parents shown us?"

I felt incapable of persuading him and I could find

no arguments, for I too have more than once longed to leave home. I have a job that I enjoy. I could live by myself in a little place that I should always keep spotless, and where I could entertain my friends, both men and women.

Olivier's mind was darting from one subject to another.

"What I cannot understand is how she got to Givry to take the train or the bus."

"She probably called for a taxi."

"She didn't. This morning I saw Léon, the fat taxi driver, waiting in front of the station. I stopped and asked him if he had called at our house to pick up a girl with a big blue suitcase. He had had no message from the house and had seen no sign of any girl with a suitcase.

"His colleague was waiting behind him and I asked him the same question. He hadn't gone to the house either. And there are no other taxis at Givry."

"It's scarcely a mile to walk."

"With a heavy suitcase!"

"Unless Mother drove her to the station or to the bus stop."

"Very likely. To make sure of her leaving the district."

"Do you promise you'll wait a week?"

"Let's say I'll wait a few days unless something happens in the immediate future."

"What do you mean?"

"I don't want any more scenes. It upsets me too

much. Afterward I feel ashamed of myself and of other people."

"Are you going home now?"

"I'll go in half an hour or an hour. I'll be there for dinner, don't worry."

I called the barman and tried to pay. My brother stopped me.

"Are you crazy? Have you forgotten you're a girl?"

Funny Olivier! I let him have his way. He walked with me as far as the parking place where he had left his bike. We parted company.

When I reached Les Glaïeuls I was surprised to find the door open, for it's usually shut. I have become so hypersensitive that I was seized with panic, particularly when I found all the ground-floor rooms empty. Not only were they empty but they did not smell of cigarette smoke, as on most other days.

The house had not been cleaned. Yesterday's papers were still in the drawing room, and there were bread crumbs on the dining-room floor.

I went up the stairs and knocked at the door of my parents' room. A voice answered, almost steadily: "Come in."

Mother was in bed; her face was far less red than yesterday at the same time. I guessed that she had decided to begin her cure. From one point of view I was glad of it, but from another I was rather frightened.

If we always refer to Mother's novena, it is because there always comes a point at which she goes to bed and withdraws, as it were, from the life of the household.

Every day her consumption of alcohol decreases slightly. I once spoke of this to Dr. Ledoux, who seemed greatly surprised at my mother's showing so much strength of will.

"In fact, she deliberately tries to dealcoholize herself. It's horribly painful, at the beginning particularly. She must keep her eyes fixed on the clock, waiting for the moment that she's set herself for a first drink, then for a second. Her entire organism must be upset. I suppose she takes a tranquilizer?"

"I don't know. One scarcely dares go into her room."

"Does she eat anything?"

"She must go downstairs when there's nobody there, for something's always missing from the icebox. She doesn't take any proper meals."

"It's so painful that I've seen cases of nervous depression and even, though these are rarer, of suicide."

Her eyes seemed to be sunk deep in their sockets. This was due to the dark shadows on her eyelids. She had not done her hair, probably not washed.

"I haven't done any housework. I've prepared nothing for dinner either, but I called up Josselin's."

This was the delicatessen at Givry, where they also sold fruit and vegetables.

"I left the door ajar downstairs, so that he could come in and put the cold cuts in the refrigerator. I've ordered eggs, too, and salad."

I could imagine the effort these simple actions must

have cost her. She probably took advantage of being downstairs to remove one or more bottles and hide them somewhere in her room.

"Go off now. It tires me to talk."

Involuntarily I glanced at the empty place beside her in the bed, and thought how, presently, my father would come and lie there. This false intimacy made me feel uncomfortable. As far as I know there has been no affection between them for a long time. They have reached the point where they can scarcely endure one another.

And yet, every evening, they undressed and slept in the same bed.

It was beyond me. It sickened me slightly, especially when I saw my mother in her present state.

She will not admit that she's an alcoholic. Officially, she is ill; she suffers from migraine headaches that make her dizzy.

"I hope you soon feel better," I said.

She turned on her side and closed her eyes.

I took advantage of being upstairs to go into Manuela's room, where I never set foot while she was working for us. The iron bed was unmade, the sheets and blankets were tumbled, which reminded me of the state my brother had been in when he last visited her.

The two of them had lain in the narrow bed, with its single pillow stained with lipstick.

On the floor I saw a shabby slipper and, bending down, I found its fellow under the bed. She must have forgotten them. The drawers were empty. On the chest of drawers there was nothing but an old Spanish magazine and a novel with a gaudy cover.

There was nothing in the armoire except a dirty pair of socks of Olivier's, and in the bathroom I picked up a broken comb.

I went down the stairs and into the kitchen to set the table. This evening there would only be three places. This would go on for about a week, which is the average time it takes my mother to detoxicate herself, after which she returns to normal life.

It distressed me, today, to see her lying in bed, so unkempt and wretched. She must have been tempted, ten times a day, to raise the bottle to her lips and drink as much as on previous days, or even more.

I knew that she despised and loathed herself; Dr. Ledoux had mentioned that too. And yet in a month or two she would begin all over again.

There was some ham, some cold veal, salami, and tongue. I put them out on a platter and washed and dressed the salad. I could find no cans of soup in the cupboard where they are usually kept. We must have used up the last.

Presently, when my father was in his study, I would go around the rooms with the vacuum cleaner and mop the kitchen floor.

My father was the first back. He, too, was surprised not to see Mother and to find me alone in the kitchen.

"Mother wasn't feeling well, and she's gone to bed."

"Have you seen her?"

"Yes. She called up Josselin's to order some food."

He had understood. He did not go up. He knew he must not. He would just creep into the room as late as possible to go to bed. Then she would at any rate be pretending to sleep.

When Father had gone to read his paper, Olivier came back and remarked with a sneer when he saw me alone:

"Don't tell me Mother's gone off too!"

I resented his harshness a little, just a very little, for I could imagine how painful the situation must be for a boy of his age.

To think that he'd been dreaming of a motorcycle, a real one, one of those hefty machines we see going past on Saturdays and Sundays with a girl behind the rider. Father, for fear of accidents, had always put off buying him one.

If poor Olivier were to leave us and join the army . . .

There; everything was ready. I told them that dinner was served. I apologized for not having had time to make soup, and I passed the platter of cold cuts to my father.

Olivier and he were still not on speaking terms; they would not even look at one another. I took the platter and passed it to my brother, who helped himself generously.

"Mother said she had eaten," I remarked casually.

They both knew what course things would take. We are so used to the fiction that we go on playing the game, even when she is not there.

"How is she?" Olivier asked.

"Not well. She'll probably be better tomorrow."

I suddenly began thinking about the Professor, who must be sitting at dinner opposite his daughter. In their apartment on the Place Denfert-Rochereau there was also an empty place at table, but there it would remain empty forever.

Unless Czimek should marry again . . .

I blushed suddenly. And I wondered if I had not just discovered the reason why, for the past four days, he had avoided looking at me.

Did he imagine that the death of his wife had raised my hopes, and that I dreamed that someday he might marry me?

This idea upset me so much that I wanted to get up, walk about, wring my hands, Heaven knows what else. It was horrible. Such a thought had never even crossed my mind.

Would he avoid me now, keep me at a distance, for fear I would claim a place in his life to which I was not entitled? He knew that he was a sort of god to me. He should have known, too, that I claimed nothing from him, except a little notice from time to time, a gesture which would imply just a little fondness. That would be enough. That is all I ask from him.

I believe that if in his turn he were to fall in love, I should be frightened. I need to give my devotion freely, without hope of return, and when he happens not to speak to me for a whole day I bear him no grudge. He has other things to think of besides a romantic girl.

Is it really romantic? Is it not, rather, human? Don't we all need to give rather than to receive?

If he had conceived the idea that I was hoping . . .

I was being sincere with myself. I knew that if he offered to install me officially in the big apartment on the Place Denfert-Rochereau, with his daughter, I should refuse. I should not feel at home there. I should be awkward and unnatural. I should feel ashamed of my love, which would no longer be freely given.

I looked at the two men at table with me. They both wore the same stubborn look, and my father was displaying no more sense than his son. Was there any hope that in a few days life would go back to normal again? We had never had any real family life, except perhaps when we were small. Almost always, each of us had lived apart from the rest, and laughter was so rare at home that I cannot remember hearing any. The fact remains that we put up with each other, more or less, especially when Mother was not on one of her drinking bouts.

Now, the feeling one could sense between the two men was almost hatred. My father was ashamed of what he had done, and he would never forgive his son for having humiliated him.

For Olivier it meant the tarnishing of his first experience of sex, of what he must consider as his first love affair.

Each in turn left the table. I cleared away, and filled the sink with hot water to wash the dishes.

Do scenes like this happen at my uncle's home, at my

aunt's? It's unthinkable that this should only happen to us, that we should be so exceptional.

Family life is not what we are given to believe, and the Professor himself, two days before his wife's fatal accident . . .

But it's not for me to complain of that, or to blame him for it.

I should so much like life to be clean and beautiful! Clean, above all, without petty hatreds and shabby compromises. People looking one another in the face, gaily, and with confidence in the future.

What sort of future was my brother preparing for himself, for instance? For I was sure, now, that he would not go on with his studies. He himself had admitted that he had only started them to please my father.

At heart he was impatient to come to grips with real life, as he said. As long as he was in the house he did not feel free, in spite of his recent outbursts.

And there must be hundreds and thousands like him, with the same vague aspirations, uncertain which path to take.

I doubted whether military service would be good for him. Here too he would have to obey and be dependent on all his superior officers, not to mention his seniors in the ranks.

I felt so miserable that I was ready to collapse into a chair and begin weeping again, my head buried in my apron.

Was my brother managing to study, alone in his room? Was it still worth his while?

I was convinced that he was afraid of becoming a failure. He wanted to assert himself, but he did not know in which direction. And I could sympathize with him, and suffer on his account.

I myself had been lucky. I might have failed my exams and been discouraged by some unfriendly teacher. I might have fallen in love with one of the boys with whom I had had intimate relations. They had not really taken me seriously. They had merely been taking what came their way, probably guessing that my main motive was a desire to reassure myself.

I put away the plates and silverware. I folded the tablecloth. I got the vacuum cleaner from the closet.

It was one of the few evenings when television voices were silent in the house, and it gave one a feeling of emptiness.

Unconsciously, I did the housework more thoroughly than I had intended. I lost count of time. I washed the kitchen floor and polished it.

At one point, when I was on my knees, I saw a pair of legs beside me. It was my father, who was watching me in astonishment.

"D'you know what time it is?"

"No."

"Half past eleven."

"I'll have finished in a quarter of an hour."

He put a hesitant hand on my head, and I was reminded of the Professor's hand patting my shoulder, at Broussais.

"I'm going up to bed."

"I'll be going up myself soon."

I had the whole of the ground floor to myself and I took advantage of it to clean my father's study.

As though I felt the need to sacrifice myself, to undergo some self-inflicted punishment.

5

My mother did not telephone the employment agency, and it was just as well. In her present state she would have frightened off any possible candidates.

I myself called up the butcher's, and then Josselin's, and told them I would go around to do the marketing, so that they should not come and ring at the door.

It was good for me, on the whole, to have something to do when I came home from work.

The Professor had resumed his routine, and he spent

over ten hours a day in the labs and in his office. His face looked sunken, his eyes were grave, and now, once again, he sometimes turned his penetrating gaze on me.

I dared not smile at him. I averted my head a little, feeling sad and ill at ease. I felt I should never shed that almost physical sadness that clung to me like a sort of fever.

On my way home I stopped at Givry-les-Etangs and bought some calves' liver, then at Josselin's I got a few provisions, bacon and eggs and butter, oranges and grapefruit; I also bought apples and pears, and I did not forget some cans of soup. I had the impression that I was being watched with curiosity and I wondered what the local people thought of us.

On the threshold of the shop I met fat Léon, who used to drive me in his taxi when I was still a child. He was really fat, but surprisingly agile. He joked from morning till night and he was a sort of local celebrity.

"Well, Mlle Laure, has that girl turned up?"

Without thinking, I asked whom he was speaking of.

"Why, that Spanish girl of yours. Seems you've lost her."

"She's gone back home."

"Unless she's gone off with a boy friend?"

That evening I did the housework again, and I went upstairs to clean out Manuela's attic. I disliked having to touch the sheets in which she had slept with my brother.

At one point I needed a rag. So as not to have to go

down two flights of stairs and up again, I went to see if I could find one in the loft, which is full of all sorts of things.

I saw a broken rifle of my brother's and a bicycle that had become far too small for him. My own old bicycle was there too, with flat tires. One day when I was riding along a footpath I had run into a tree and Dr. Ledoux had to put several stitches in my scalp. And there were our old tennis rackets with broken strings.

I went to the far wall, bending down, because the roof slopes steeply, and I was surprised not to find the old green trunk in its usual place.

It had always been there, full of old linen and bits of stuff, and I don't believe it had been used for traveling since I was born. It must have belonged to the time when my father was serving in Algeria and moving about fairly frequently from one garrison to another.

I found nothing that I could use as a duster, and I went down to the kitchen to get one.

When I went to bed the two men had already gone upstairs. I fell asleep almost immediately.

Next morning, when I took Mother her coffee, I found her rather poorly, as I had expected. It was the second day of her cure, and one of the most trying. She was staring more fixedly than ever, as if the world around her did not exist and as if her whole attention was concentrated on what was going on inside her.

She was pressing one hand against her chest, which was being shaken with painful spasms.

A few years ago this had horrified me, and I had thought she must be dying. Now I am used, like the others, to seeing her in this state.

"Have you taken your medicine?"

"Yes."

"It'll pass off in an hour or so."

Especially when she had had a good swig of liquor. Her entire organism was protesting against the enforced deprivation.

"Do you know what happened to the trunk that was in the loft?"

"What trunk?"

"The one that used to stand against the far wall. A green trunk with a yellow band around it."

She sighed as though in pain and I had the impression that she was playing for time. It seemed cruel of me to ask her so futile a question when she was in such distress.

"I don't remember. It must be so long ago. . . . Wait a minute. . . . A secondhand dealer came by one day with his cart; he was traveling from house to house and from farm to farm buying up junk. I took him up to the loft. I know I sold him a table with a broken leg and the two rush-bottomed chairs. He must have taken the trunk too. Nobody used it any more. It was a long time ago."

No, I had seen that trunk in the loft less than a year ago when I went up to get something there one day.

What worried me was the fact that my mother felt the need to lie. I went to have my bath and then I rode off to Broussais, where everything seems clean and clear and where, unlike what happens at home, not everyone is trying to conceal something.

Because of the trunk, or because of the cleaning I had done the previous day, I kept thinking of Manuela and I tried to imagine her lugging her suitcase of imitation leather as far as the station or the bus stop. There was something phony about that explanation.

In the afternoon I asked Mlle Neef for an hour's leave and I went to the Avenue Paul-Doumer. I found an expensive-looking apartment house, built of limestone, with very high windows through which one could perceive molded ceilings. In the lodge there was no mere concierge but a uniformed porter.

Moreover, the word "lodge" is hardly adequate to describe the miniature drawing room I glimpsed through the glazed door.

"M. and Mme Lherbier, please. . . ."

I had got their name from my brother. A smoothly running elevator, with velvet-lined walls, took me to the second floor. I rang, and after a fairly long wait the door was opened by a girl who answered the description I had been given of Pilar: she was small, thin, and swarthy, with huge dark eyes and a ready smile.

"Whom did you wish to see?" she asked.

Her tiny apron and her cap were made of embroidered batiste.

"I would like to speak to you a moment, mademoiselle."

"We're not supposed to have visitors."

"Might I perhaps ask leave of your employer?"

"I don't know whether . . ."

She had the same accent as Manuela but spoke better French. She must have been in France for some time.

A door opened. A woman appeared, dressed in a mink coat, ready to go out.

"Pilar . . ."

The girl went up hurriedly and I saw them whispering together, looking at me. Mme Lherbier finally came toward me.

"What is it you want, mademoiselle?"

"I apologize for intruding in this way. Our maid is a compatriot of Pilar's and a friend of hers. She disappeared a few days ago and I wanted to make sure nothing has happened to her."

"Pilar! You may answer this young lady's questions if you're able to."

She made sure, with a rapid glance, that nothing was missing from her crocodile-skin handbag and left the apartment.

"When did you last see Manuela?"

"Wednesday last week."

"Did you spend the afternoon with her?"

"Yes. It's my free day. In the morning I sleep, and in the afternoon we look around the shops, Manuela and I, or else we go to the movies. We went to the movies. Then she had a date, but we met again afterward."

"Did you have dinner in a little restaurant on the Avenue de Wagram, where you often go together?"

"How did you know?"

There was a seat covered with green velvet and we sat down on it, Pilar somewhat hesitantly.

"Manuela told us she nearly always dined there with you before going dancing at Hernandez's."

"That's right."

"And did you go to Hernandez's?"

"Yes."

"You've got many friends there?"

"I know nearly everyone. They're all Spaniards there, including the waiters and the band. My boy friend plays in the band. That's why I always stay there till closing time."

"And Manuela? Did she have a boy friend too?"

"She had a lot of friends."

"Do you mean lovers?"

"She often changed boy friends, don't you see? She liked having fun, Manuela did; she wasn't the sort to stick to one man."

"How did she get home to Givry?"

"Sometimes by the last bus. Or else one of the gang might have a car. That's how it was last Wednesday. There were five or six of us, including José. José's the musician. We all piled into a little car and we sang all the way."

"Was Manuela in good spirits?"

"Just as usual."

"She never talked of leaving her job?"

"No. She was quite happy. She was always happy."

"She had no intention of going back to Spain?"

"Surely not. Her mother died ten years ago. Her father has a tiny plot of land and she had to look after her seven brothers and sisters. She'd always dreamed of coming to Paris. When she got her papers she ran away from home, for her father would never have let her leave."

I was trying to visualize a somewhat different Manuela from the one I knew.

"Did she tell you about my brother?"

"Olivier?"

"You even know his Christian name!"

"He's quite young, isn't he, and rather innocent. She said he'd never made love before and was terribly afraid of making a fool of himself."

She laughed, a throaty laugh like Manuela's.

"Did he want to marry her?"

"Well, he swore it was serious, and he tried to make her promise not to go dancing at Hernandez's. . . . He was jealous. . . ."

"And my father?"

"She told me what happened. It was very funny."

"Why?"

"I'm sorry. You know, Manuela didn't take anything seriously, and we always told each other everything."

"Did my father suggest her leaving our house?"

"Yes."

"He wanted to set her up in a little apartment, didn't he?"

"I didn't dare mention it. With him, too, you'd have thought it was the first time he'd had a mistress."

"She didn't accept?"

"Of course not."

"Why?"

"It's hard to say. It couldn't lead to anything, you understand?"

"Weren't you surprised at not hearing from her?"

"Yes."

"What did you think?"

"That she'd got a new boy friend. That perhaps she'd changed her job."

"You're sure she never spoke of going back to Spain?"

"Never!"

"Did she talk to you about my mother?"

"She's not . . . she's not like other people, is she?"

The word "crazy" was on the tip of her tongue.

"Doesn't anybody at Hernandez's know any more than you do?"

"I only went back there yesterday. They were surprised to see me alone. I knew already that she'd left Givry."

"How did you find that out?"

"We used to call each other up about every other day. I got your mother on the line eventually and she told me Manuela had left for Spain. I said to myself that was an excuse she'd given for leaving her job."

"Wouldn't she have let you know?"

"I can't understand it."

"You were really close friends, weren't you?"

"She used to tell me everything. I was the only girl

she knew in Paris. As for boys, she used to laugh and joke and make love with them but she wasn't going to tell them what she was thinking about."

"Thank you, Pilar."

"Are you worried, mademoiselle?"

"I don't know. She may have had her own reasons for disappearing. My father's proposal was rather tempting."

If I had not felt so remote from the Professor I might have talked to him about it and he would have advised me. I didn't dare. As for the other lab assistants, such problems have never entered their lives.

I became increasingly uneasy, and I was somewhat ashamed of it. I told myself again and again that I was imagining things, that I tended, like my mother, to dramatize everything.

If Mother was waiting to finish her cure before calling up the employment agency, I had a full week of cooking and housework ahead of me.

Mother was still not eating proper meals and she was always in bed when any of us got home. Only when she was alone would she come downstairs, unsteadily, and get something to eat out of the icebox. And also, no doubt, take a fresh bottle from her hidden store. It was odd that we had never discovered where she kept it; she was amazingly cunning in this respect.

I went up to see her when I got home, after stopping at Givry again to buy meat and vegetables. She was not reading. Neither was she sleeping, although her eyes were closed.

"Is that you?" she murmured faintly.

"Yes. How are you feeling?"

"Not well."

"Have you been in much pain?"

She did not answer. Surely it was obvious!

"Has nobody come?"

"I didn't hear the bell."

"And no phone calls?"

"No."

"When Pilar called up . . ."

"Who's that?"

"A friend of Manuela's."

"A Spanish woman telephoned. She wanted to speak to Manuela. I replied that she wasn't here any longer. The woman wanted to know where she'd gone and I said she'd gone back home."

"You're sure Manuela told you that?"

"Yes. I'm not in the habit of lying."

That was untrue. She lies instinctively. Or else she distorts the truth so much that you can't recognize it.

"Did she call a taxi?"

"I don't know."

"You didn't hear if she called up Léon or the other taxi driver?"

"No. I wasn't feeling well. I knew your brother would make a scene."

"And Father?"

"Your father too. Men are crazy. As soon as a girl comes into the house they're after her like flies."

"You didn't drive her to the station or to the bus stop?"

"No. That would have been the last straw! She wanted to go, and it was her own business how she did so."

My mother seemed to have recovered a certain energy.

"I told you I hadn't been feeling well. I went upstairs and lay down. I believe I heard the door bang. I was having a bad attack."

I could not tell how far she was lying, but there was certainly a false ring about her story.

"Why do you ask me such questions? Isn't it bad enough that I'm laid up in bed, that your father and brother aren't on speaking terms, that we've got no one to do the work, and that I'm alone in the house all day?"

She spoke with more bitterness than ever.

"You needn't be afraid; I shall soon be better. In a few days you won't have to bother with anything. I shall do the housework until I can find somebody."

I was disappointed and slightly sickened. She managed, God knows how, to make me feel guilty. I had just time to prepare dinner and tidy up downstairs a little. My father found me setting the table and gave me a vague greeting as he made for his study.

"Father."

"Yes?"

"I want to ask you a question. It's very important. Forgive me for meddling with what's none of my business. You offered to keep Manuela in an apartment in Paris, didn't you?"

"Who told you that?"

"Her friend Pilar, from whom she had no secrets."

"And you believe those two girls?"

I looked him in the eyes, my lips trembling, for I felt unsure of myself and this was the first time I had confronted my father in this way. It was strange. I was looking at him somewhat as I might look at a stranger and I had a feeling that he was being evasive, that he, too, was evasive, prepared to lie.

"I believe them."

"And what if it were true?"

He was humiliated, unhappy, searching vainly for a dignified attitude.

"You would be within your rights, of course. Your private life is no business of mine."

He was staring at the floor.

"What I need to know, because it concerns us all, is what has become of her."

He said nothing. He waited.

"You didn't come back and fetch her to take her to Paris?"

"No."

"You didn't pick her up somewhere on the way?"

"No, I tell you."

"And you haven't any idea where she can be?"

"Your brother's the person you should ask. Or your mother, who's quite capable of having thrown her out."

"Thank you. . . ."

Father was not being frank with me, either, and Olivier surprised us in an embarrassing tête-à-tête. He looked at each of us in turn, mistrustfully. At home, now, no one trusts anyone else.

"Aren't we going to eat?"

"Are you in a hurry?"

"Yes. I've got a date with a friend."

He never tells us anything about his friends and they never come to Givry. Is it because he is ashamed of Mother? There's a whole side of his life of which we know nothing. He comes and goes, leaves the house at different times, comes home to dinner or not, sometimes goes up to bed without saying good night to us in the drawing room.

Perhaps it's just a naïve way of proving to himself that he is independent?

"Whom've you been out with, Olivier?"

"Some fellows."

"From the Science Faculty?"

"Maybe. I didn't ask them."

"Haven't you made any friends there?"

"Most of them are snobs. Or else, like us, they live some way out of Paris."

"Don't any of them come from Versailles or the neighborhood?"

"I couldn't say."

I did not know whether he went to dance halls, whether indeed he knew how to dance. As for meeting prostitutes, that was quite out of the question.

"I've seen Pilar."

"Where?"

"At her work place. I saw the lady she works for too."

"What for?"

"Her employer happened to be just going out. She let me ask her maid a few questions."

"What did Pilar tell you?"

"Just what she told you. She doesn't believe that Manuela has gone back to Spain. She might have said so in order not to admit that she was tired of working for us."

"She'd have told me."

"You're sure of that?"

"Certain."

I was less certain than he. A few minutes later we were sitting together at the round table, in silence.

I started doing the housework, as on previous days. But I was still worried about Manuela's disappearance and suddenly, about ten o'clock, I decided to go and see what I could find out at Hernandez's. My brother was out. I knocked at the study door and announced to my father:

"I'm going out for an hour."

"Don't forget your key."

It was not raining, but it was cold. When I got to the Avenue des Ternes I had to ask my way. The first few people I spoke to did not know the place. Then a policeman told me:

"About a hundred yards farther on, on the left, between a shoeshop and a pastry cook's, you'll see a blind alley. It's down that."

I left my motorbike on the avenue and ventured down, looking rather unfeminine in my parka. The dance hall advertised itself in blue and red lights, and in front of the door a few men, in small groups, were smoking cigarettes and hurling epithets at the women who passed by. They were all speaking Spanish. Most of them wore brightly colored shirts.

Some of the women they addressed answered in the same vein. Others blushed and hurried through the door. A big globe hung from the ceiling, made of tiny fragments of looking-glass which reflected the light of the spotlights. This globe revolved slowly over the heads of the dancers, casting luminous patches on their faces and on the white walls. There were two rows of tables around the floor, with paper napkins on them.

Almost all the places were filled and, having taken my bearings, I went up to the bar, where only a few men were standing.

"May I have a fruit juice?"

"Surely," replied the barman.

He winked to the others. I was no doubt the only Frenchwoman in the hall, and they exchanged jokes in their own language.

"Do you know a girl called Manuela Gomez?"

"Si, señorita. Yes, mademoiselle."

"Is she here?"

"Is it Wednesday?"

"No, Thursday."

"She only comes on a Wednesday, with Señorita Pilar."

Each of his remarks was greeted with laughter or smiles from the other men.

"Did she come yesterday?"

"What d'you mean?"

"Yesterday was Wednesday. Did they both come?"

"No, mademoiselle. Only Señorita Pilar."

I could not tell what was so funny about his answers. It must have been his tone which sent them all into fits of laughter. We seemed to be putting on some sort of comic turn.

"Don't you know where she's gone?"

"Señorita Pilar?"

"No, Manuela."

I was beginning to lose patience.

"Oh, you mean Manuela. A fine girl, Manuela."

"Does anyone here know where she's gone? Did she have a boy friend?"

"Many boy friends, mademoiselle."

He pronounced it *mademezelle*, and stressed the word each time.

"Many, many boy friends."

"I mean, did she go with anyone in particular?"

"Lots of people in particular."

It was impossible to keep it up. I should learn nothing, and they were laughing at me more than ever.

"Dance, mademoiselle?"

"No, thank you. I must go."

I paid. They tried to keep me back.

"A glass of Spanish brandy?"

I answered just anyhow and edged my way back to

the door. Now I only had to dodge the small groups outside.

I had learned nothing more than I knew when I arrived, except that Manuela was very popular at Hernandez's and that she was not shy with men. I had already guessed as much. When I reached the corner of the alley I almost collided with someone who was striding forward, and just as I opened my lips to apologize I recognized my brother.

"What are you doing here?" he asked, but he had certainly guessed the answer.

"Trying to get news of Manuela."

"Did you find out anything?"

"No. They made fun of me. She wasn't here yesterday."

"Are you worried?"

"I don't know. I'd feel easier if I knew where she is. I don't like all this mystery about her departure."

"D'you know what I've been doing?"

"No."

"For the past two days I've cut my lectures and I've followed Father from morning till night. I think he's bound to look her up at some point and that this is the only way to find out her address.

"So far he's merely gone to his office, lunched by himself in a small restaurant nearby, gone back to work, and then come home."

"Has he noticed you following him?"

"I don't think so. And even if he should notice I don't

care. Things have got to such a point between us
now . . ."

"Are you going to Hernandez's?"

"I was going there. I may as well look in there on the
chance, though I don't expect I'll be any luckier than
you."

"Don't drink too much."

"I've drunk nothing today but one glass of beer."

"Goodby."

"Goodby."

We did not kiss each other. We have never gone in
for demonstrations of affection at home. And yet my
brother and I are very fond of one another. I worry a
great deal about his future, and I should so much like
him to be happy!

If it weren't for that girl . . .

Now I had begun thinking like my mother, and
laying the blame for everything on Manuela. Was it the
girl's fault if Olivier had made love to her, and should I
hold it against her that she had granted him the pleasure he begged for?

My father's case was rather different. She might
have . . .

Why? I tried to put myself in her place. I could still
hear the barman's voice, the laughter of the men
standing around the bar. I had got the impression that
practically all of them had been on fairly intimate
terms with her.

She was gay. She loved life. She loved love. She
wanted everyone to be happy. . . .

Why not my father, who had forgotten his dignity and begged for love, too?

No. I hadn't the right to blame him. It was the atmosphere of the house that was responsible.

I was at a loss. I wanted to stop thinking about it. My father had gone upstairs when I came home, and I did a little more housework before going to bed.

Next morning I felt tired and listless. As usual, my father came down first to have his breakfast and he cast a surreptitious glance at me.

"Aren't you feeling well?"

"I'm tired."

"We ought to start looking for a maid. You can't go on doing everything."

"There's no point in engaging one until Mother has recovered."

"How is she?"

He had slept beside her but they had not exchanged a word. Last night and this morning she must have kept her eyes closed, so that he had to inquire after her health from me.

"She's feeling badly. The first three days are difficult."

"Is she eating a little?"

"She goes down to take something out of the refrigerator. She waits until I've left the house."

"Has she spoken to you about Manuela?"

"I questioned her."

"What did she say?"

"That she knows nothing. Just what she told us the

first day. That Manuela had told her she was going home."

"Do you believe her?"

"No. I've seen Pilar, her friend. Pilar assured me that Manuela can't possibly have gone back to Spain. . . . She ran away from home because she had to look after her father and her seven brothers and sisters. She never had a free moment."

"What can have happened to her?"

Just as my father was asking me this question as if he were putting it to himself, I happened to think of the green trunk. I was on the point of mentioning it.

I didn't, however. I felt I was making up a sinister story and my father would merely shrug his shoulders.

My brother came down next.

"Did you have better luck than I did at Hernandez's?"

"I'm still wondering how I managed to get away. I went up to the bar. I spoke about Manuela and they all burst out laughing. I had to restrain myself not to lose my temper, for I couldn't have fought a dozen of them by myself. Anyhow, I'd have had the whole roomful against me. They told me a young lady had been asking the same questions, and they kept nudging one another."

"The young lady was me."

"So I gathered."

"I must hurry if I'm to catch up with Father. It would surprise me, actually, if he visited her so early in the morning."

"I think you're on the wrong track, Olivier."

"I'm beginning to think so too. Now that I've begun, I want to carry on to the end. I may as well do that as go to classes that I don't intend to follow through."

My colleagues must have noticed that I had been rather gloomy the last few days, but they were mistaken as to the real causes of my depression. In the cafeteria, however, I tried to join in the conversation of our little group.

It was at about five o'clock that I was suddenly made very happy. I was working in the lab when somebody stopped behind me and I started on hearing the Professor's voice.

"I shall be needing you presently. Don't leave."

I turned around, trembling with gratitude, but he went off without looking at me. It didn't matter. He was in touch with me again. He had asked me to stay.

I counted the minutes and found it very difficult to concentrate on my work. When the six o'clock bell rang most of my colleagues went off to change before leaving. A few of them stayed on to finish some job.

It was not until half past six that I found myself alone in the small laboratory, where Czimek soon joined me.

"Have you checked on Joseph?"

"Yes."

"His pulse?"

"Normal."

"Blood pressure?"

"Still the same."

"Bring him out, will you? Can you hold him by yourself?"

"He's used to me."

"It looks as if there's been no rejection. . . ."

He dared not yet express satisfaction, for the success of this experiment was something he had hardly dared hope for. Stethoscope in hand, bending over the dog, he went on speaking in the same tone of voice:

"I've missed you a great deal."

I dared not say anything.

"I did not expect you to turn away from me as you have done."

"I turn away? Was that what you believed?"

"For over a week you've stopped looking me in the eyes and you never come near me."

"Because I daren't inflict myself on you."

"You're speaking the truth?"

"I've been miserable all this time. I didn't seem able to come near you. I thought you were annoyed with me."

"About what?"

"I don't know. I might have wearied you."

"Put the dog back into his cage."

He followed me with his gaze, and his face was grave.

"I can't quite believe that I was mistaken. You see, it's in moments like those I have just been through that one feels the value of true friendship."

In spite of myself, I burst out fervently:

"I wanted so much to . . ."

"What?"

"I don't know. To comfort you. No, that's too pretentious. To surround you with a little human warmth. I thought of you all the time. I imagined you alone with your daughter."

He looked at me in surprise, still somewhat incredulous.

"Is it true that . . ."

He held out both hands and took mine, clasping them so strongly that it hurt.

"Thank you. I believe you. It's funny. We were each wrong about the other. It won't happen any more."

He was tactful enough not to kiss me, but to leave things as they were, looking at me with a sort of gratitude and saying with an assumed fatherliness in his voice:

"You must be hungry. Hurry home to dinner."

"What about you?"

"This evening I've got a report to write. I've brought a sandwich and a thermos bottle of coffee."

I did not offer to stay. I knew that when he was writing a report he liked to be alone and even his secretary was not allowed into his room.

"I hope the work goes well," I said.

My eyes and my whole face were alight with joy. A sense of relief pervaded my entire being and I ran lightly down the stairs instead of taking the elevator.

A misunderstanding! There had been nothing more than a misunderstanding between us. Each of us, as he had pointed out, had been mistaken about the other.

I was still thinking about it as I rode out of Paris on my motorbike. An idea suddenly occurred to me. If a misunderstanding of this sort had arisen between the Professor and myself, it might also arise between other people, it must certainly arise hundreds of times every day.

Could I be sure that this was not what had happened between us and my mother? I say us, because I knew that my father and brother more or less shared my feelings.

All her attitudes, whether she was on a drinking bout or not, irritated us. For a long time now we had considered her mentally sick, even if only to a slight extent, and I had several times seriously thought of consulting a psychiatrist.

Might she not, like the Professor, have been waiting meanwhile for a gesture or a look from us?

I had not dared look him in the eyes. I had been afraid he might think I was glad to see a vacant place beside him. That would have been monstrous of me. I had stayed aloof, waiting for a sign.

And he, meanwhile, had been hoping for some encouragement from me.

He had finally had the courage to speak out and the misunderstanding had vanished.

Had we ever talked frankly with my mother? Had

we told her what was worrying us? Hadn't we treated her as if she were outside the family?

It was because of her, more or less, that I had never brought friends home and that Olivier invited nobody to the house. As for Father, he never saw anyone.

We were ashamed. We expected her to be disagreeable or eccentric.

Didn't she know this? Had she not understood it and resented it, long ago? Was this not one of the reasons for her drinking bouts?

We left her alone all day. We rushed off in the morning, one after the other, on our bicycles, and only rarely did one of us go home for lunch. And in the evening we would sit down at the table without asking her how she had spent the day.

After which Father would shut himself up in his study, and my brother would go out or up into his room.

Who had begun it? I pondered the question seriously, but it all went back too far into the past for me to find an answer.

If it was all due to a misunderstanding, my thoughts about her were all wrong, and I felt remorseful. I wanted to give her a chance to live with us, as though in a real family with trustful, affectionate relations between its members.

The Professor had clasped both my hands, looking me full in the face, and his eyes, though still sad, were full of compassionate affection. I was happy. I wanted everyone to be happy.

When I got home my father and brother were at the table, eating an omelette. In the kitchen I noticed some soup plates.

"Who prepared the meal?"

"I did," muttered my brother as though he were confessing a sin. "I opened a can of pea soup and broke half a dozen eggs in a bowl."

"Has anyone been up to see Mother?"

They each looked at me in turn as if to say that they had not thought of doing so.

"I'm going up to see if she needs anything."

I went upstairs, knocked, and opened the door. She was sitting up in bed and watched me come in with an impassive face.

"What do you want?" she asked. "Have you come to spy on me again?"

"No, no. I came to see if you needed anything."

"I don't need anything."

"Has nobody come? Has nobody telephoned?"

She said with a sneer: "I forgot that even when I'm ill I'm supposed to watch the house."

Her eyes were hard, her voice full of rancor. I felt that it must have taken years of disappointment to bring her to this state.

Had she ever been happy? Even as a child, she was teased by her brother and sisters about her ugliness.

Were those people so very far wrong who said that my father had married her chiefly because she was his Colonel's daughter?

Had she suspected this from the beginning? Or had her eyes been opened in the course of time?

I had lived with her ever since I was born, and I had suddenly discovered that I did not know her. When I was able to judge her, or rather when I took it upon myself to judge her, she had already become what she was today and I had no way of discovering the past.

"Aren't you hungry, Mamma?"

"You know quite well that when one's in pain one is not hungry."

"Is there nothing I can do for you?"

Obviously I was not being very clever. One cannot change one's attitude overnight, or in the course of a day.

"What's come over you?" she asked sarcastically.

"I've been thinking of you a lot today."

"Really?"

"I've been thinking that we leave you alone too much."

"Well, now I'm asking you to leave me alone."

"I want to tell you, too, that I do love you."

"For heaven's sake!"

I felt I had better go away. I was doing her more harm than good. I was being tactless and ridiculous.

"Good night."

She did not reply. She lit a cigarette. Over her nightgown she was wearing her housecoat of a faded blue that intensified the darkness of her hair and eyes.

She would not be really ugly if . . .

I had to stop thinking. My ideas were growing hopelessly confused, and I went down into the kitchen to make myself an omelette.

My brother went upstairs, my father into his study, and mechanically, as my mother usually does, I switched on the television.

6

The Professor did not speak to me again or ask me to stay on after hours, but our eyes met several times during the day. I felt that a sort of complicity had arisen between us, together with a certain peace of heart.

I know that whatever happens to me and whatever happens to him, no man will ever fill his place in my life. I ask nothing from him. That is perhaps what gives me the greatest sense of exaltation. I should like to be the one who gives, while he simply accepts.

My colleagues have known for a long time that there's something between us. They exchange knowing looks when they leave in the evening and see me stay behind, and they involuntarily glance ironically toward the little room where the cot stands.

They have understood nothing and I don't hold it against them. Still less do I feel the need to explain to them something that is a very simple truth. As a child I used to watch processions go by, men and women following the Holy Sacrament holding lighted candles, and I remember seeing some faces lit up with total joy, eyes oblivious of surrounding reality and fixed on some vision beyond the reach of other people.

I felt somewhat like those believers and I calmly braved the mocking smiles of my companions.

Did Czimek realize the place he filled in my life? Could he possibly be aware that my devotion was absolute and that without it I should cease to exist?

I had entered love as others enter the Church, and that is why, no doubt, I no longer really belonged at home. I prepared breakfast, I cooked dinner, I tidied up and swept. These were only external gestures which formed no part of my inner life.

Today, again, I stopped by at Josselin's to buy something for dinner, and there, rather to my surprise, I saw Mme Rorive, who was gossiping as she did her marketing. She fell silent as soon as she caught sight of me, and I suspected that she had been talking about me or my parents.

149

"I'm so glad to see you. There's nobody ill at home, I hope?"

I haven't the gift of second sight, but I could swear that she was only there because she knew that for the past few days I had been stopping by at the same time, on my way back from work.

"My mother isn't very well."

"Is she in bed?"

"Yes, but it's nothing to worry about. Her usual migraine headaches."

"Oh, that's so painful! I have a sister who suffers from them too, and when they come on she doesn't dare even cross the road."

She had finished her purchases. Her shopping bag lay on the counter beside her but she made no attempt to leave.

She was dressed in mauve, her favorite color, probably because she thinks it looks distinguished. Her white hair has a mauve tinge too, and her complexion is mauve with a faint trace of rouge on her cheeks.

"Will you give me four jars of *rillettes*, four slices of pâté, and two dozen eggs."

"You know, I was a bit worried. Today, for the third time, I called at your house with M. Rorive and nobody answered the bell."

Like many tradespeople who have spent much of their lives behind the counter, they referred to one another by their surnames, preceded by Monsieur or Madame.

"Have you lost your maid?"

"She has left."

"Will that be all, Mlle Le Cloanec?"

"Would you add a little parsley?"

Mme Rorive left the shop with me.

"Won't you come and have a cup of tea or coffee and a little piece of cake with me?"

There is a pastry cook's opposite, with small white tables around which the ladies of the neighborhood have their cakes and gossip. I was feeling uneasy about what she had said of her three visits to our house. She is almost as familiar with our habits as we are ourselves, for she spends much of her time peering through her curtains. She was well aware that my father and brother would not be back for another hour.

I followed her resignedly.

"Tea or *café-au-lait*?"

"Black coffee, please."

"A slice of fruit cake?"

"Thank you."

"I ought not to eat cakes, because I'm fat enough as it is, but I can't resist them. She was Italian, wasn't she?"

"Spanish."

"With a funny sort of name. Foreigners nearly always have funny Christian names."

"Manuela."

"Yes, that's it. A girl who was always laughing, a pretty girl who must have had plenty of lovers. . . . And from what I saw of her she can't have put up much resistance."

"I don't know what she did on her days out."

"I remember recently, about a week ago, she came back very late in a car. I wasn't asleep. Sometimes I can't go to sleep and I'd rather sit up. It was at least two o'clock in the morning. There was a whole gang of them piled up in the car with her, singing at the tops of their voices."

"How do you know it was she?"

"I heard the car stop in front of your house, and then your front door shutting. That's why, when I didn't see her again, I thought your mother had probably got rid of her."

"She went home to Spain of her own free will."

"Couldn't she get used to life in France?"

"I don't know."

"Has your mother sent for Dr. Ledoux?"

I did not immediately get the drift of her question. "Why?"

"Because dizziness and cold sweats are often due to catching a chill."

I still could not understand. What did she mean about catching a chill? I was convinced that for all her apparent naïveté Mme Rorive's remarks were never pointless.

"I did think, that night the dog died, that she was unwise to go out in the rain without even putting on a warm coat."

I asked involuntarily: "What dog?"

"Didn't your mother tell you? She probably didn't want to upset you. It was on Tuesday or Wednesday.

Wait a minute. On Tuesday, because I could swear we'd had soles for lunch. It's the day we have fish.

"It doesn't matter. What I'm certain of is that it was raining. Not the heavy storms we'd had the week before but a cold drizzle.

"I was waiting for M. Rorive, who had gone into town to do some shopping. I was by the window watching for him, for I'm always worried when he goes off driving by himself."

I felt distressed for no precise reason. It seemed to me that this chatter concealed a danger as yet unknown, and to keep my composure I drank a mouthful of coffee.

"Aren't you going to eat your cake?"

"Yes. It looks very good."

"You can't find anything like it in Paris. Where was I? It was some time after dark. A car drove up from the Givry direction, very fast, with its big yellow headlights lighting up the wet road.

"Suddenly, in the shaft of light, I saw a big dog I'd never seen before. It looked like a stray. It was walking in the middle of the road and the car didn't have time to brake. If I didn't hear the bump, I felt as if I'd heard it.

"I'm much too fond of animals to see an accident like that without being upset. The car went on its way while the dog, which had been practically tossed into the air, fell down more or less on the spot where it had been hit."

I was increasingly puzzled as to why Mme Rorive

felt impelled to tell me this story. She was conscious of my interest, and enjoying it inwardly.

"I was so bowled over that I poured myself a tiny glass of crême de menthe. I was drinking it in the living room when M. Rorive came home. I said to him:

" 'We might perhaps go and say hello to dear Mme Le Cloanec. I made some raisin bread this morning. I might take her a loaf.'

"I know your mother adores it. I once took her one and she told me how she enjoyed it."

Was all this true or untrue?

"I took my umbrella. M. Rorive wouldn't take his, saying it wasn't raining hard enough and that his raincoat was enough. You can imagine my surprise when I noticed that the dog was no longer on the road. I was sure it was dead. The way it had fallen down, in a broken heap, it couldn't have failed to be dead."

She went on talking, talking, but without neglecting her cake.

"M. Rorive rang the bell. The ground floor was all dark but there was a light on upstairs in your parents' room. You see I've got to know the house! When you've got only one neighbor . . ."

How I wished she would come to the point!

"Well, for the third time, nobody answered.

" 'Perhaps she's in the kitchen and doesn't hear?'

"We didn't yet know that your maid had left. I was a bit worried and M. Rorive said:

" 'Let's go and knock at the other door.'

"We went around the house and knocked at the back door. There was no light in the kitchen either.

" 'Just leave your raisin bread on the doorstep.'

" 'The rain will soak it.'

"Then, I know it was cheeky of me but you must forgive me, I tried the door handle. The door wasn't locked and it opened. I put the loaf down on the table in the passage . . .'"

"But the dog? I don't see what the dog has to do with . . ."

"I'm coming to that. Wait a minute. Just as we were leaving I heard a noise coming from the direction of the wood. The moon had just appeared and I saw your mother coming through the garden gate. She had no coat or hat on and she was pushing a wheelbarrow. . . ."

"Was there anything in the wheelbarrow?"

"No. We didn't wait for her, for fear she might be annoyed to see us there. I suppose she must have seen the dog on the road too. She must have come down to find out if by any chance it was only hurt. Then, finding it dead, she must have thought of throwing it into the pond with a stone tied to its neck. . . ."

Her tone suddenly altered. "What's the matter with you?"

I replied stupidly: "With me?"

"You've turned quite pale. You're fond of animals, aren't you? I'm sure you'd never have left the poor thing lying in the middle of the road, just under your windows."

"I must go back and cook dinner," I said.

"It's nearly dinnertime. Of course you're only having cold things."

She had noticed what I was buying at Josselin's. She insisted on paying our bill.

"It was my invitation. Did you have some of my raisin bread, by the way?"

"I believe . . . Yes. . . ."

Actually, this was not true. For one reason or another, my mother had never mentioned a loaf of raisin bread. But then of course she had been in the middle of her novena.

What had she done with it? She had certainly not eaten it herself, because when she is drinking she cannot bear anything sweet. Had she thrown it into the garbage can? Why should she?

What had been her reaction on discovering, when she came back from the ponds pushing a wheelbarrow, that somebody had been in the house?

I went home. Unlike the evening of Mme Rorive's latest visit, the lights were on downstairs. There was nobody in the drawing room, nor was there in the dining room, where the table was set.

In the kitchen I saw my mother, who had got dressed and was standing very upright, too upright, as though to prevent herself from collapsing.

"You've come down?"

She looked at me without answering and heaved a long sigh. I would not have expected her to be capable of coming down today. It was not the first time I'd had evidence of her prodigious strength of will. She was walking about in a jerky, mechanical fashion.

"I've brought something for dinner. There was a pâté just out of the oven and I took four slices."

I laid my purchases on the table. The sight of food must have turned her stomach but she gave no sign of it.

"Aren't the men back yet?"

"I'm all alone."

There are moments when I admire her as much as I pity her. She is alone, indeed, even when the three of us are at the table with her. She lives in a world apart, which we do not know, and we have grown used to ascribing her behavior to eccentricity or to drink.

Perhaps because a few glances from the Professor, that day, had made me happy, I felt a little closer to her, or rather I wanted to be closer to her, to tell her that I understood her, that I knew how wretched her life had been.

Weren't we all a little to blame? I stared at her and felt like crying. I imagined her in the rain, coming back from the wood, from the ponds, going through the narrow gate at the bottom of the garden, whose rusty lock has ceased to function, and pushing the wheelbarrow she had taken from the shed.

Involuntarily I asked her:

"What exactly happened about the dog?"

Her eyes suddenly narrowed and she stared at me with such intensity that I felt ill at ease, and looked away.

"What dog?"

"The one that was run over by a car in front of the house. A big stray dog walking in the middle of the road."

I looked up. Her lips had gone white. She must be suffering horribly and I felt ashamed of being unkind, just as I had felt ashamed the night when my father had been humiliated by Olivier. I think humiliation is what hurts a human being most.

"Who told you about a dog?"

"Mme Rorive."

My mother could see that I was terribly upset. She undoubtedly guessed what I was thinking, and I expected her to crack up, to let slip what I might call her mask.

To my great surprise, however, she held firm. I said casually:

"And what about the raisin bread?"

"What raisin bread?"

"Mme Rorive came in by the back door and left a loaf of raisin bread on the table in the passage."

"I never saw any raisin bread in the passage."

And my mother added a little phrase that astonished me:

"That woman's mad!"

My brother's arrival put an end to our conversation, and Mother began putting out the cold meat on a plate.

"Well, you're up already?"

We are all cruel to her. We ought not to seem surprised at her having got up and trying, by dint of an astonishing effort of will, to resume her place in everyday life.

"Come here a minute, Laure."

He went into the drawing room. This, again, is something we ought to avoid, these conversations in corners, lowered voices, whispered remarks. How can she possibly feel at home? How can she not believe that she is different from other people?

"What do you want to tell me?"

"That I've made my inquiries. I can join up in January, with the new draft, and by anticipating my call-up I'm entitled to a choice of service."

"You're still thinking of that?"

"More than ever."

And, with a vague gesture toward the kitchen: "You've seen her, haven't you? Do you think I'm going to go on living in this atmosphere?"

"She's being brave."

"I'd sooner she had stayed in bed. Don't say anything to Father yet. I'll try to get my call-up papers and at the last minute I'll ask him to sign."

"Suppose he refuses?"

"He won't refuse. After what has happened, my presence here embarrasses him and he'll be relieved not to have me in the house."

"*What dog?*" she had asked, her face ashen.

And then her final remark: "*That woman's mad!*"

These two little phrases haunted me all through the meal. Father, as stiff as ever, pretended to ignore Olivier's presence. Isn't it possible that with time all this antagonism may lessen and perhaps eventually disappear?

Opposite me, Mother was toying with her food, and I saw her hesitate to pour herself a second glass of red wine, although she was obviously in need of it. So I helped her at the same time as myself, and she looked at me in surprise, but without the least gratitude.

"What dog?"

"That woman's mad!"

I muttered: "Excuse me." And I left the table. I hurried up to my own room, reaching it just in time to give vent to the sobs that were choking me.

The dog . . . Mme Rorive . . .

"She told me she was going back to Spain."

I wanted to be with the Professor, very close to him, and to tell him everything, ask him what I ought to do. I felt hot and cold at once. I lay there with my face buried in the pillow, and I sobbed without even thinking about what was making me so unhappy.

I had a terrible nightmare from which I literally wrenched myself, forcing myself to wake up, and for a long time I stayed sitting up in bed, gasping, incapable of distinguishing accurately between my imagination and reality.

In the dream, I had not gone to the hospital and my presence had clearly worried my mother. It was raining. It must have been dark outside, for the lamps were alight in the house.

The two men had gone off, Olivier on his motorbike, wearing his parka, and Father in the car.

We were both sitting in the kitchen, Mother in her pale blue housecoat, over which she had tied an apron. It was four minutes to nine by my alarm clock. Then three minutes, then two minutes to nine. I don't know why I felt compelled to wait until exactly nine o'clock.

My mother was afraid. She stared at me with enormous eyes and asked:

"What are you going to do?"

I waited to answer till the hand stood at the center of the dial and I said:

"To make you speak. I've got to know."

I was calm. I was conscious of fulfilling a task imposed on me by Fate.

"I swear there's nothing to know."

"The dog?"

"There never was any dog."

"The dog in the middle of the wet road?"

"Mme Rorive is mad."

"And the wheelbarrow?"

"I never used the wheelbarrow."

"What did you do in the wood?"

"I never went into the wood."

Her face was distorted with anguish and she was wringing her hands.

"And Manuela's imitation-leather suitcase?"

"She took it with her."

"Where?"

"To Spain."

"She didn't go back to Spain."

"She said she was going to."

"You're lying."

"I am not lying."

"I insist on your telling me the truth, and I won't repeat it to anyone."

"There's no truth to tell. What are you doing?"

It was a cry of terror, for I was moving implacably toward her.

"Don't hit me."

"I shall hit you if I have to. I want you to tell me what you've done with Manuela."

I was holding her by both wrists and they were as fragile as the wrists of a child, with a very soft smooth skin.

"Don't hurt me."

"Then tell me."

"I've nothing to say."

"You killed her."

She did not answer but gazed at me with wild eyes, her mouth open for a cry that never came.

"Tell me why you killed her."

"She took everything from me."

"What did she take from you?"

"My son and my husband. She taunted me, she made fun of me because I'm not a gay person."

"You were in the kitchen together?"

She did not answer but looked around her as if she had forgotten where she was.

162

I don't know at what point he had come in, but the Professor was there, in his white lab coat and cap. He had heard everything, even though I had only just caught sight of him. He was shaking his head sadly and looking at me as if he wanted to make me understand something.

Only I could not understand. I knew that I had a job to do, and I was doing it.

"What did you strike her with?"

She struggled a little longer, trying to free her wrists from my firm grip. She muttered at last, turning to glance at the table with its brown and white checked oilcloth:

"The bottle."

"You struck her with the bottle?"

She nodded.

"Which bottle?"

"The bottle of wine."

"Was it full?"

"I'd drunk a little."

"You were drinking out of the bottle when she came in? Was that why she laughed at you?"

"She laughed at me and I hit her."

"She fell onto the ground?"

"She was staring at me with her big round eyes and walking toward me. The bottle was broken. I took the rolling pin which was lying on the table and I hit her again."

"Several times?"

"Yes."

"Did she fall down?"

"No."

"Did she stand there a long time?"

"Yes, a long time. And I kept on hitting her. She began to bleed from the nose and mouth."

"And then she fell down?"

"Yes."

"Did you know she was dead?"

"Yes."

"How did you know?"

"I knew."

"And the dog?"

"There hadn't been any dog yet."

"What did you do?"

"I went to get the trunk out of the loft."

"So you hadn't sold it to the junk dealer?"

"No."

"You lied to me?"

"I always lie. I can't help it."

"What did you want to do with the body?"

"To throw it into the old pond, but I didn't want it to float to the surface. I took the old rags down into the cellar."

"Are they still there?"

"No. Next morning, after you'd all gone, I put them in the garbage pail."

"Did you take her pulse?"

"No. She was dead."

She repeated, as though reciting the responses in church:

"She was dead."

"You put her in the trunk?"

"Yes."

"You picked up the bits of broken glass and wiped away the stains of wine and blood?"

"There was hardly any blood."

"You went to get the wheelbarrow?"

"Yes. It was raining."

"Did you put on your coat?"

"No. I wasn't cold."

"Were you able to carry the trunk by yourself?"

"I dragged it. I'm strong. Nobody believes that I'm strong, but it's the truth."

"What did you put into the trunk so that it wouldn't rise to the surface?"

"A shoemaker's last that was lying in the shed and your father's old vise."

I had dropped her wrists and she kept on speaking in a monotone like a schoolchild reciting a lesson.

"Where did you throw her?"

"Into the old pond. At the place where there's a hole. I'd heard it said that the mud there is over a yard deep."

"Were you strong enough?"

"I was strong enough. The hole is close to the worm-eaten little jetty."

"And suppose the jetty had given way?"

"It did not give way."

"And the dog?"

"I came back and I went upstairs to wash my hands."

"Was there a loaf of raisin bread in the passage?"

"No. I saw the dog out of the window."

"So there was a dog?"

"Yes."

"Why did you bother about it?"

"I don't know. I didn't like having it in front of the house."

"Didn't it occur to you that if you'd been seen with the wheelbarrow it would serve as an alibi?"

"I don't know. Why are you so unkind to me?"

"I'm not unkind. I shall have to live with the memory of this from now on."

"So shall I."

"It's not the same thing."

"Why not?"

"Did you go and fetch the wheelbarrow again and put the dog in it?"

"Yes."

"What did you put around its neck?"

"An old piece of an iron grating."

"Did you throw it into the old pond?"

"Yes."

"At the same spot?"

"No. At the place where the two ponds join. There's a sort of channel with a little bridge across it."

I know that my face was relentless and frightening, and she kept staring at it in terror. The silence made it even more terrible, for I could think of no more questions to ask her.

"You mustn't tell anyone, Laure. Promise me not to tell anyone."

And as I did not answer, she went on in a little girl's voice:

"I won't do it again. I promise I won't do it again."

I turned to look for the Professor. He was standing in the doorway. And as I gazed at him with questioning eyes, he nodded to me.

What did he mean? That I must promise? He looked serious and severe. I think he was not pleased with me. He had not spent years in our house and he did not know my mother.

"Don't tell anyone, Laure. I don't want to go to prison. I don't want them to shut me up!"

And then she gave a final cry: "I tell you I'm harmless!"

I must have cried out too, as I wrenched myself out of sleep, out of my nightmare. I did not immediately think of switching on my bedside lamp, and I sat there in the darkness, listening to the rain beating on the shutters.

I had difficulty in getting my breath back, and for a moment I even wondered where I was.

It had been so real! It had seemed so true! Was it possible that . . .

I listened, to find out whether my cry might not have wakened my parents and whether anyone was coming. No. The whole house was asleep. I was bathed in sweat. I reached out to switch on the lamp.

I don't know why I stammered under my breath: "The dog."

I could not tell what was true and what I had invented. I got up and went to drink a glass of water in the bathroom. I decided to take a sleeping pill so as to sleep heavily and dreamlessly.

When I woke next morning at the usual time I was so tired that my first thought was to stay in bed and call up the hospital presently to say that I was not feeling well.

But my dream immediately came back to me, with my mother and myself in the kitchen after the men had both left.

I did not want to stay alone in the house with her. I should have been capable of questioning her, of insisting, at all costs, that she should tell me . . .

I took a shower, dressed, and went downstairs. I found her making the coffee.

She looked at me and said: "I don't need anybody."

"I didn't know whether you were down. We'll have to phone the agency to get a maid."

I was appalled to find how like she was to the woman in my dream. She had on her pale blue housecoat, which in fact is what she usually wears, and she had tied her apron over it. The illusion was so strong that I turned to the table to look for the rolling pin.

"What do you want?"

"Nothing."

I felt I had better leave the room. However, I poured

myself a cup of coffee and took it into the drawing room, where I automatically started tidying up.

I dared not admit to myself that what had disturbed me most was the attitude of the Professor. He had looked at me sadly, as if he were disappointed in me. I'd felt that his eyes were telling me not to go on, not to try to find out.

My forehead was bathed in sweat again, and I was relieved when my brother came down and went to take his usual place at the table.

I joined him, as though to put myself under his protection. He was surprised to find Mother serving his breakfast. She said only this:

"Good morning."

He looked at me and was surprised to see me in such distress.

"What's the matter with you?"

"I had a horrible nightmare."

"And is that what's reduced you to this state?"

That remark was enough to show me how hard it was going to be. I wanted to answer, to tell him everything.

But I could not tell anybody anything. I had promised. Had I really promised? It was impossible to be left this way between dream and reality.

"Will you go with me as far as the hospital, Olivier?"

"Why? What are you frightened of?"

"I don't want to feel alone."

He looked at me curiously as he ate his breakfast.

"I've never seen you like this."

"If you'd lived through my dream . . ."

"One doesn't live through dreams."

"While a dream lasts it's as real as reality."

"Where did you read that?"

Then my father came down and we both fell silent. I was conscious of the passing minute, of our family life, of four human beings together in a suburban house.

My mother was a pale blue figure in the kitchen, drinking her coffee out of a big bowl that we generally use for beating eggs.

My brother had nearly finished eating and was still in his shirt sleeves. My father, fully dressed, was eating his toast and staring straight in front of him.

And I was looking at all three of them. I felt I was looking at myself too, seeing myself there among them, and my face seemed all puffed up.

The minute passed and there were more minutes, and there will be many more.

"Come on, then!" my brother called out, getting up and putting on his jacket.

He went to get his parka in the hallway. He waited for me to put on mine and my rubber boots, for it was still raining.

We walked across part of the yard, along the gravel path, to get our motorbikes.

"You really won't tell me anything?"

"I've nothing to tell you, Olivier. I assure you it was only a bad dream."

"I've got a feeling you're hiding something from me."

"I'm a bit blue this morning."

"And yet Mother's fairly well. I expected her to stay in bed at least two days longer. She's never recovered so quickly from a novena."

"You're quite right."

Why had she made such an effort? Wasn't it because in real life, too, she was afraid?

We rode on side by side and went through Givry, past Josselin's, past the bakery. Today I would have no need to stop and buy food. I was sure that Mother would order things by telephone, as she always does when she is not on a novena.

I felt a little calmer now that I was out of doors. The rain lashed my face and sometimes took away my breath. My brother adjusted his speed to mine and we reached the road that runs from Versailles to Saint-Cloud. The sky was so gray that it seemed as if daylight had not yet broken, and we put on our headlights. So did the other people making their way to Paris like ourselves, some on motorbikes, some on bicycles, some under cover in their cars.

From time to time Olivier turned to look at me. He seemed anxious. He was not used to seeing me give way. At the corner of the Boulevard Brune a sullen crowd was emerging from the entrance to the métro station, and my brother waved to me before going on his way.

I reached my destination. I was back in the light,

whitewashed rooms, among the long tables crowded with test tubes, spirit lamps, and gleaming instruments.

I went to put on my white things like all the rest, and almost automatically I assumed my professional expression.

7

We met two or three times during the first part of the morning, but we did not work together. I tried hard to put on a brave face, realizing how woebegone I must be looking. I felt that he was puzzled, that he was trying to understand, and I hated myself for adding to his worries.

About eleven o'clock he was no longer to be seen in any of the labs, and a little later his secretary came to tell me that he was asking for me in his room. The furniture there was of mahogany, with brass hardware, and the walls were almost entirely covered with photographs of leading medical personalities from all over the world.

In this over-solemn setting he appeared smaller, thinner, almost insignificant. It seemed as if he were trying to adapt himself to his surroundings, and he was not the same man as in the lab.

"I didn't want to question you in front of your colleagues. Please sit down."

He motioned me to the chair in front of his desk, and I felt ill at ease there, as if I were a visitor.

"You're not well, are you?"

"I hardly slept all last night, and the little sleep I got was very disturbed. I apologize for appearing in such a state."

He looked at me affectionately, trying to understand.

"Have you got family worries?"

"Yes, particularly about my mother."

I should have liked to tell him everything, to confide in him entirely, but I felt I had not the right to do so. He had just endured his own tragic experience. He had barely recovered from the blow that had fallen on him.

"She has always been rather unbalanced, and at times I wonder if she would not be better off in a psychiatric hospital."

"You're sure it's as serious as that?"

I could not tell him that I was convinced she had killed someone. I had no proof of it. And I was still under the influence of my dream. Wasn't it absurd to attach so much importance to that?

"What do the doctors say?"

"She has always refused to be examined by a specialist. My father dared not send for one against her will. As for our family doctor, he ascribes her eccentricities to alcoholism."

"Does she drink a great deal?"

"Yes, periodically. For several days she goes on drinking practically all day, in secret. She's fiendishly clever at getting hold of alcohol and hiding the bottles all over the house, so as to have one available at any moment. Then she goes to bed complaining of migraine and only leaves her room when there's nobody else in the house.

"She eats nothing at mealtimes. She nibbles secretly at whatever she can find in the refrigerator."

"How is her health?"

"She complains of those migraine headaches. In fact she suffers from them only when she is drinking. At such times she lives unsteadily in a nebulous world, and I'm always afraid she may commit suicide. She must be particularly tough, for at forty-seven she has never been ill. Dr. Ledoux thinks that her troubles are imaginary."

It did me good to speak, to see him listening to me and trying to form an opinion.

"She was unhappy as a child. She thought she was ugly, and the fact is that she hasn't an attractive face.

Now she's so thin that you wonder how she can keep on going."

He wanted to help me. It was the first time he had asked me about my family, and I had to restrain myself not to tell him all about Manuela, Olivier, and my father. I'd have had to describe the atmosphere of our house.

I was ashamed of taking up his time, of stealing his sympathy.

In any case, how could I confide in anyone, even in him? It was not my secret; it was my mother's. I could keep silent, at least I supposed so, for I am her daughter and I cannot be required to denounce her.

But could somebody else? Could he? I did not know the law; I believed, however, that anyone who knew of a crime was bound to inform the authorities.

I refused to put him into such a delicate situation. I could not accept the idea of making him my accomplice.

I had had a nightmare, because of a few remarks of Mme Rorive's about a dog and a wheelbarrow. That nightmare clung to me and I still found it hard, so many hours later, to feel sure that it had not really happened.

Why should Manuela not have left of her own accord? She had only been with us two months. We knew little about her, and nothing about her real character, except that she went to bed with all and sundry, gaily, because that was her nature.

And because one evening I had come home and found her not there, was it reasonable to condemn my mother?

I was torn between contradictory feelings.

"It's done me good to be allowed to talk to you. I'm grateful. Please forgive me, from now on, if you see me looking downcast or preoccupied. Don't take any notice of me, will you?"

"You don't want to confide in me?"

"For the moment it's impossible. Everything depends on what happens."

"I won't press you."

"Will you let me take the afternoon off?"

"Of course. Take a few days' leave if it's any help."

"It would be worse to spend all day at home."

I said good-by awkwardly, as though I scarcely knew him except as the big chief that he is. I went to the door and there turned back for a moment. Why did I get the impression that he was looking at me as though in a dream? His eyes seemed to be trying to send me a message that I could not understand.

I did not want to lunch in the cafeteria, under the curious gaze of the other lab assistants, nor did I want to go home to eat, so I went to the little restaurant where I had gone to drink brandy one evening and to which I had subsequently returned with my brother.

I ate at one of the small tables with red tablecloths and the barman turned on the phonograph. A soft, subdued music filled the room.

I was not hungry. I felt utterly lost. If I'd been told the police were coming to arrest me I'd have believed it.

However, I eventually ate something and I even took a dessert, which I seldom do.

When I reached home there was nobody on the ground floor and I was seized with an irrational terror. And yet it was quite natural that my mother should have gone to lie down in her room.

I kept on my rubber boots and my parka and, under the drizzling rain, I went out by the back door toward the gate at the bottom of the garden.

The trees were almost completely bare and the ground was thickly carpeted with sodden leaves. Nobody went through these woods in winter. A hundred yards from our house a track ran from the road to the big pond, but we always used to take a short cut along a scarcely visible path.

I am ashamed to admit that I was looking for the marks of the wheelbarrow. There were none, needless to say, among the dead leaves. I followed the bank of the big pond as far as the wooden bridge that crosses a sort of narrow channel joining the two ponds.

Here there were no leaves, and on the muddy soil the traces of a single wheel were still clearly visible. Some rushes had been flattened and even broken as if a heavy, bulky object had been pushed over them.

No landscape had ever seemed to me so sinister, and I have never felt such a sense of loneliness. The rain made little rings on the surface of the pond and the trees stood out blackly against the low sky. I felt cold in spite of my parka. I wanted to talk to someone.

And I suddenly realized that I should never be allowed to talk.

I went back, hesitantly, toward the house, thinking about my father and Olivier and what attitude they would take if they knew the truth. Did my father not suspect it? If he did, as I believed, he must be unwilling to learn it, preferring to remain in doubt.

As for my brother, I believed him to be incapable of keeping a secret like this one. He would go into the army as he had decided. And it was probably better for him.

I felt really cold. I had to make an effort to stop my teeth from chattering. My mother had heard me come in. Was she watching me from a window?

I stopped in the shed where the wheelbarrow was kept, and I made out some fresh scratches on its sides.

A pile of old iron had always stood in one corner and I could have sworn that this pile had dwindled, I could see neither the rusty vise my father had used in the days when he used to tinker about the house, nor the cobbler's last.

I felt lost and utterly alone in the midst of a hostile universe and I was afraid to go back into the house.

I did not have the heart to condemn my mother. I felt that we were all guilty, we who had let her gradually sink into an abyss of solitude and despair.

I thought I saw the curtain stir over the kitchen window. I could not remain outside indefinitely. Nor could I go back to town and wait to come home until my father and brother were back.

I pushed open the door with a reluctant hand, pulled off my boots, hung up my parka on the coatrack.

Mother was there, standing in the kitchen, three yards away from me, looking at me with a fixed stare.

8

I went forward, and I was no longer cold or frightened. My mother was not a threatening figure, and her gaze expressed only her own terror.

I had the impression that in her eyes I figured as a judge and that her life depended on me. She did not speak. She had nothing to say. She waited.

And I said, in as natural a voice as I could manage:

"I didn't feel well and I left the lab early."

That did not explain my visit to the wood or to the

shed. It explained nothing but my evident distress. In spite of myself I gazed at her intently as if I wanted to understand everything. She was so pitiable with her flat chest, her clothes hanging loosely about her, her long thin neck and pointed nose.

It was as if I fascinated her. She stood as motionless as an animal on the alert, with only an occasional quiver of the nostrils.

What was the good of telling her that I knew? She was conscious of that, and she was waiting for my verdict. So I said casually:

"I wonder if I haven't caught a chill."

What would they do with her? Would they send her to prison for the rest of her days? Or else, on the grounds of diminished responsibility, would they shut her up in a mental hospital?

She seemed shrunken with fear. I had never before lived through or even imagined minutes like those I then endured. It seemed to me that the world had stopped turning, that it had ceased to exist, that there was nothing but the two of us face to face.

If they tried to shut her up anywhere my mother would kill herself, I'm convinced of that. Was this a solution? Was it the only one?

I rejected it. And I knew that by holding my tongue I was assuming a heavy burden, that I was making myself responsible for my mother.

I had dreamed of a tiny apartment in Paris where I should be alone, in my own home. I had imagined that someday, much later, Czimek would come to visit me there and that he would have his own armchair beside the fire.

I realized now that I should have to stay here, to look after her, to avoid fresh tragedies.

I would be the only one to know, alone with the bare, horrible truth.

What was the good of putting questions to her, of asking if things had happened as I had dreamed?

She was surprised to hear me say:

"I feel like drinking something to warm me up. A hot toddy, for instance. Is there any rum in the house?"

She spoke at last, under her breath, as though talking to herself.

"I believe there's a bottle in the cellar. I'll go and see."

I put some water on to boil. There are some familiar gestures that one performs unawares at the most painful or dramatic moments. You put on water to boil, you set out two glasses, two spoons, some sugar, a lemon.

It was untrue that I needed to warm myself up. It wasn't possible to stay any longer face to face in silence.

The rum represented a sort of absolution, a promise that there would never again be any mention of Manuela, who had loved life so much. Had not her gaiety, her greed, been a kind of insult to my mother?

And then my brother, shamelessly, had visited her room; my father, barefoot, had crept up to the second floor to listen behind the door, and then had taken her to a shady hotel.

Manuela took everything!

Had she really surprised my mother in the kitchen that day, drinking red wine out of the bottle, and had she laughed at her?

I would never know.

What was there left for the woman who now came upstairs with a bottle of rum and poured some into the two glasses? She was ashamed, she had been ashamed all her life, ashamed of being ugly, ashamed of her drinking bouts and of the tremors that seized her when she stopped drinking.

I would never speak to her of what had happened between her and Manuela, even if it meant that I should never know the real truth myself.

She had guessed that I knew. It was not the same as uttering the words.

I poured boiling water into the glasses. Neither of us wanted to sit down. I should have felt as if I were paying a call.

But from now on I would always be here. From time to time the Professor would keep me after work at the lab. None the less I would become an old maid, like my aunt Iris, except that I should not have a place of my own, a little apartment that would reflect my personality, as Iris had her apartment on the Place Saint-Georges.

"Inspector, I have come to tell you that my mother . . ."

It was unthinkable. It would be monstrous. And yet

she was still shaking. She could not believe that her nightmare was over.

I pictured men dragging the pond and bringing up the green trunk.

"Drink up," I said, seeing her hesitate.

Heavens, how fragile she seemed, how insubstantial! I found it hard to realize that she was my mother.

And though I felt bitter toward her for forcing me to make this decision, I had not the heart to condemn her.

The rum sent a warm glow through my chest. My mother must have felt her legs giving way, for she sat down on the edge of a kitchen chair, as if she dared not take a more comfortable seat.

"Did you call up the agency?"

"Yes."

"Have they got anyone?"

"They'll call me back tomorrow morning."

Under my eyes, year by year, my mother had gradually become an old woman.

And I, slowly but surely, was going to become an old maid.

She was looking at me, still watching but already with a gleam of gratitude.

She was no longer utterly alone.